Anything is Possible

Anything is Possible

Rob Osborne

The Book Guild Ltd

First published in Great Britain in 2017 by
The Book Guild Ltd
9 Priory Business Park
Wistow Road, Kibworth
Leicestershire, LE8 0RX
Freephone: 0800 999 2982
www.bookguild.co.uk
Email: info@bookguild.co.uk
Twitter: @bookguild

Typeset in Minion Pro

Printed and bound in Great Britain by CPI Group (UK) Ltd, Croydon, CR0 4YY

ISBN 978 1911320 685

British Library Cataloguing in Publication Data.
A catalogue record for this book is available from the British Library.

MIX
Paper from responsible sources
FSC® C013604

I would like to dedicate this book to my late father.
I've achieved something that can never be taken away from me. Love u pop xxx

Acknowledgements

I would like to thank my wife for her love and support all of these years xxx

My two children, for endless hours of enjoyment.

Cheryl B, for giving me the belief that ordinary people can get a book published.

Alexia, for proof reading my manuscript. When I quickly read your first letter, I thought the book was rubbish because I saw 'Totally rewrite'. Thankfully, it was for only one chapter.

My sister, for reading the latest amendments.

I would also like to thank people in advance for buying the book. I hope you like it and if you want a sequel, who knows, *anything is possible*!

1

He stood there transfixed, staring at the magazine. It was her Abbey Jones. The soap star. God, she was beautiful! Her beauty paralysed Matt. Unable to pick it up, all he could do was stare at the front page, motionless.

"Are you gonna buy that, or stare at it all day!"

The voice distinctive, he spun round to see the familiar tall, lean frame of his best mate.

"I was waiting for the last copy so I could get it before you and torment you with it! Good weekend, Bully boy?"

"Nah, same old shite! Went to pick up Johnny and got my ear chewed off by Sandra."

Bully, real name Jim, was divorced. One of these young marriages that failed, but not before producing a son, whom he idolised.

There were endless arguments between the two of them. Bully wanted more access to his son and Sandra would not budge. He felt that she was being deliberately awkward to punish him in some way, as if Bully was the cause of the break up. The truth of the matter was that he fought like mad to keep the relationship going. There was nothing more he could have done.

Even now he resorted to living in a dingy bedsit to ensure Johnny wanted for nothing. Matt had lost count of the number of times that he had offered to put Bully up in his spare room. Each time he refused, citing that he didn't want them to be known as sad gits. Not only was he extremely generous he was immensely proud.

"She's after more money again; don't know how she expects me to afford the current amount, bitch!"

"Come on, I'll buy you a coffee at work," Matt replied.

"Coffee's free," Jim responded, looking puzzled.

"Well you can make it then," Matt smiled. "Best get to work or Sandra will really give you a hard time."

Matt took one last look at the magazine, finally picked it up and made his way past a handful of people reading magazines to the checkout where he handed it to the young female cashier, who put it in a bag. They then trundled off to work, weaving their way through the morning crowds.

After a short walk they met the rest of the employees waiting to enter the premises of the Grand Bank. This was one of the worst parts of the job, waiting outside for someone to carry out the morning security check. Especially on cold days like today. Everyone was trying to keep warm by either walking around or snuggling up inside their coats.

Bully pulled a set of keys out of his pocket, "Is anyone in there?"

"Yes, Julie, about five minutes ago!" replied one of the girls, shivering.

Just then a figure appeared at the door, smiling. This was the signal that it was safe to enter. A posse of cold staff members hurried to the door practically fighting each other to get out of the cold first. Once inside they scattered, like ants leaving the colony, some preparing to start work, some off to the toilet to reapply makeup or relieve themselves and others going upstairs to make tea. Matt and Bully did their usual, straight upstairs to sit in the staffroom.

Once upstairs Bully threw his coat on a table, receiving scowls of displeasure from the staff members already sitting there.

"Give us a look, then!" he said, snatching the bag out of Matt's hand.

"I thought you were making the drinks?" retorted Matt.

Bully's eyes remained trained on the magazine. "You can do it!"

Matt tutted as he walked over to the kettle; filled it with water and asked if anyone else wanted one and waited. All of a sudden he felt dizzy and grabbed the work surface to avoid falling over.

Bully noticed Matt swaying out of the corner of his eye and leapt from his seat.

"You OK, Matt? asked Bully "You're as white as a sheet!"

"Yeah, must have moved too quickly!"

Bully laughed loudly. "That's a first!" He returned to his seat, happy that Matt had regained his balance to resume reading the magazine whist Matt finished making the drinks and distributed them.

"Can I have my magazine back?"

"Hold on a minute," he grunted, "I've got to admit mate, she's gorgeous!"

Bully closed the magazine, slid it across the table into Matt's clutches and sipped his hot tea.

Matt stared at the pictures, analysing every last detail. He sighed.

His concentration was abruptly broken by the sound of a familiar angry voice.

"Are you two going to do any work today?"

It was Julie Grant, the manager. She stood menacingly at the door, hands planted firmly on her hips.

One warning was enough. They practically leaped out of their seats and rushed down the stairs. Julie chuckled quietly to herself, they were pushovers. She sauntered over to the table where the magazine lie and glanced down at the cover. "She's pretty," she murmured.

Abbey Jones was a young actress, who got her big break as a seductress in a soap, primarily concerned with young adults at college. Her first scene saw her driving into college in a red, sporty Mazda. Since her debut, she had managed to sleep with half of the male cast, who were only too keen to oblige. Who could blame them? She had, straight, blonde, shoulder-length hair; a body that looked well exercised, and not out of place in the Miss World contest; and long thin legs, always visible as she wore short, tight skirts. She was most men's fantasy.

Looking this good, she never seemed short of famous partners. She had dated fellow actors, sportsmen and most good-looking men from society, which probably gave the impression that she was just like her soap character – this was unjustified. They wanted to look good having her on their arms and use her as a sex object. As she was not always willing, she was often cast aside for someone that was.

Her current flame seemed no different. It was Pat Keane, one of England's finest young footballers, making his living with one of the top Premiership clubs and, of course, England.

He was very high profile, a media target, never out of the spotlight and always hounded from dusk till dawn. Paparazzi camped outside his house and relentlessly followed him. He had a boyish charm and was exceptionally good looking, making him all the more marketable for sponsorship deals. All these factors meant other women would be only too willing to throw themselves at him, much to the annoyance of Abbey.

She had a break from filming. The current storyline had her visiting parents after a bereavement, which meant she could kill two birds with one stone: see Pat play in London and visit friends.

Abbey met Pat at her friend Sonya's flat, before he was due to travel back after a hard-fought victory against Arsenal: 2-1. He had produced a match-winning performance, scoring both goals, the winner a spectacular twenty-five-yard strike in injury time.

"You were brilliant, hon. That last goal was the best I've ever seen!" Abbey said.

"Not bad, scored some better. Look, Abbey," Pat said, "it's not working out, is it?"

"What do you mean, Pat?" Abbey countered, 'déjà vu' setting in.

"We hardly see each other," Pat responded. "Not much of a relationship, is it?"

"What you mean is, I won't spread my legs at your beck and call!"

"No, not at all."

"Bullshit, Pat!" Abbey countered angrily. "So that's it, then?"

"I guess so."

"Well piss off then!" Abbey shouted.

Pat looked at her angrily and then stormed out, slamming the door behind him. Abbey began to sob; Sonya came over and hugged her.

"I think I'll stay celibate from now on!" Abbey spluttered, fighting back the tears.

"No change there, then!" Sonya replied laughing. "Let's go out tonight, you need a laugh."

"I'll need to go to the bank, then." Abbey said, pulling herself together.

"I'll also need to raid your wardrobe."

"Be my guest." Sonya smiled. "I've got to nip out for a while, just leave me something different."

She collected her coat from its place on a peg next to the front door and made her exit. Almost immediately there was a knock on the door. Abbey looked over to the sideboard and spotted the front door keys. She raced over to pick them up and placed the hoop on top on her finger and opened the door to find Sonya standing there looking sheepish.

"Every time, Son!"

She grabbed the keys from her finger, smiled and continued on her way. Abbey backed into the door to shut it. Leaning back against it, her face dropped. She was now alone.

She glanced towards the bedroom and slowly headed in and towards the wardrobe. She slid open the mirrored doors and peeked in. The choice was vast. Luckily for her they were very similar in height and weight. In fact the only noticeable difference being Sonya had dark hair and a permanently tanned skin from frequent trips to the tanning salon. Borrowing clothes was a regular occurrence.

In spite of her exhaustive efforts Abbey just couldn't find anything she fancied, no matter how hard she tried. She gave in. Feeling thoroughly depressed she slumped back onto the bed. Maybe a shopping spree might cheer her up. *Yeah right*, she thought.

Back at the bank, Matt and Bully had been watching the clock. It had been a quiet day and they had spent most of it reminiscing and recounting stories about their college days.

The remainder of the staff were left in fits of laughter, as usual. They were the office comedians. When they started, no one, including customers, could avoid the minimum of a smile.

College is where they first met and struck up an instant rapport, annoying the teachers with childish pranks and sharing a passion for music. They both adored soul music, especially Hall and Oates, going to concerts as often as possible. They both played instruments: Bully the lead guitar and Matt the piano. They would often play at college discos, but even though people thought they could make it, they were terrified of failure. Bully's romance killed off their chances, as he devoted his time to Sandra. This didn't seem to bother them. It just produced a convenient excuse.

They sat watching a staff member out in the lobby busily restocking the leaflet racks whilst another member unenthusiastically picked up litter that had been discarded during the past few hours. The last hour generally dragged and customers were few and far between, presumably more intent on travelling home than sorting out their finances.

"I'm so fucking bored!" Bully grunted. "Not even any nice birds to chat up either."

"Good job too, you'd only frighten them off," Matt laughed. "I've got to go to the bog again."

"Jesus Christ, Matt! That's about the 20th time today," Bully snapped.

"You've not got that mag in there have you?"

"No, but feel like shit."

"You mean 'feel like a shit'!" Bully joked. "Actually, you look very pale."

Matt went upstairs. He had not told anyone, but he had been feeling giddy most of the day, and nearly passed out a couple of times whilst on the toilet. He had also been reading all about Abbey since first seeing her on telly. He had dreamt about her on numerous occasions, but, being a realist, he knew that he probably would never meet her and she would definitely never fancy him. Little did he know that was about to change…

2

After endless hours of moping about, Abbey resigned herself to purchasing a new outfit. Glancing at her watch had caused panic. The time was 4.10pm. By the time she reached Oxford Street it would only give her over an hour to find something. A feat that was almost unheard of.

She charged out of the flat and spent the next ten minutes hailing a cab. To make matters worse whilst sitting in the cab she found that her credit cards weren't in her purse. She must have left them in Sonya's flat. By the time she reached her destination her mood had altered from depression to anger and frustration, which was shortly going to get worse.

Abbey arrived at the cashpoint, placed her card in the slot and it immediately spat it back out. She tried again. Same result. She looked at her watch: 4.50pm. She would have to go into the branch. She hated that. There were usually snotty women or blokes drooling. But she had no choice. She entered: no queue. *Well that was a relief*, she thought.

There only appeared to be one cashier serving and he was preoccupied. Grunting to vent her displeasure she marched up to Bully's position. He was getting ready to pack away his money, when he noticed someone standing at his till. He looked up and nearly fell off his seat in shock when he saw who was standing there.

"C-c-can I help you?" he stuttered.

"The bloody machine won't accept my card!" Abbey responded angrily.

Just then, Matt returned from his bathroom break, saw who was at the counter and stopped abruptly. Dropping his magazine, he could scarcely believe his eyes.

The sound of the magazine falling to the floor caught Abbey's attention. She saw Matt standing there gaping.

"What's up with you, never seen a woman before?" snapped Abbey.

"Sorry," Matt said sheepishly, "I've just been reading about y—"

"And you think I'm so sensitive, and would it be too much trouble to autograph it for you?" Abbey interrupted. "I suppose you want me to sign it across the tits, everyone else does!"

"Would you mind?" Matt said, by now blushing profusely. "I mean, er, anywhere will do, doesn't have to be the tits."

Bully laughed, getting an intense look from Abbey. "Now what can I do for you, Miss Jones?"

"Apart from stopping mentally undressing me, you can give me £1,000."

It was Bully's turn to blush. "I'll need to see some identification as it's over £500."

"No, she doesn't. I'll vouch for her!" Matt answered. "You arse!" he whispered to Bully.

He speedily carried out the transaction and counted out the cash. Abbey snatched it from his grasp and left, muttering about them.

"I'll need to see some ID!" Matt remarked in a silly voice. "You've blown your chances there!"

They both exploded into fits of laughter. It was 5pm: closing time.

Abbey phoned Sonya and told her she was going shopping and would see her in about an hour. By now, it was pitch-black and there was a fog closing in. Abbey shivered and headed for the first clothes shop.

Inside the bank it was mayhem. Everyone started rushing around in a vain attempt to make a quick getaway. This was usually ruined by Julie and her ritualistic rant about daily targets. Thankfully, today, her message was brief. More effort needed! She must also have a prior engagement.

Matt dragged Bully to the pub, The Swan, run by Terry. God knows how he managed to make a living. Most of the time the pub had about five customers, except on karaoke night, once a week. The pub itself was off the main track, down one of London's side roads, and was immaculately presented, both inside and out. The interior was almost entirely decked out in oak: all of the tables, the bar and the floor. Even the ceiling was covered with oak beams; it was a pub right out of the eighteenth century. Also, it had a piano in the corner of the room where people used to gather in the war and sing their troubles away.

The pub as quiet as usual with only a handful of

customers strategically scattered around the room, enjoying a quiet drink and conversation. Congregating at the bar were the half a dozen regulars, who regularly stopped in for a few drinks after work, chatting to the landlord. Terry was in his late fifties, with the slightest hint of a Geordie accent, having hailed from Newcastle originally. He moved to London in the early '70s to make his fortune. No one knew if he had.

Matt was very fond of him because Terry helped him get over the loss of his father to cancer four years ago. He was always on hand with good advice, like all publicans. He knew that the lads sang and was forever badgering them, without success, to get them to sing on his karaoke nights.

"All right lads? Another busy day?"

Two lagers appeared at the bar, both of which were quickly finished.

"I'm off! Need another row with Sandra to top my day off!" Bully smiled. He waved goodbye and left.

"Was it something I said?" enquired Terry.

"No, he's just getting a hard time from Sandra about money," sighed Matt. "Women, who needs 'em!"

"Obviously you do! Anyone on the horizon?"

"You are joking! Who wants to date a short, fat, bald bloke?"

"You're not that short, and you're stocky, not fat. Some women find baldness sexy."

"I've yet to meet one. All the girls say I'm more like a brother to them. Do you know the last time I got laid?" Matt could not contain his anger; Terry shook his head. "No, neither do I. I just get comments like 'lovely eyes' and 'you're so funny'!"

"You are!"

"God damn it!" Matt smashed his fist down on the bar. "I want a relationship that's meaningful. That's all I ask."

Terry poured him another drink. Matt wandered over to the piano and started to play. Terry looked over in amazement: in all the years he had been coming to the pub, he had never played.

The tune was fantastic! It sounded like a ballad, although Terry did not recognise it. The rest of the pub stopped to listen, obviously thinking the same. Matt stopped.

"What's the matter with you lot? Never heard a piano before?"

"Where did you learn that? Who's it by?" Terry asked.

"Wrote it myself."

"It's bloody marvellous! You've got talent!"

"If I had, I wouldn't be working in a stinking bank!" Matt replied sharply, downing his drink. "One more for the road."

The drink was dispatched equally as quickly as its predecessors. Matt apologised for his downcast manner and made his exit.

The thick layer of fog made visibility difficult and the bitter wind put a chill through the air. Matt was feeling dizzy again. Refusing to believe that there could be anything wrong the blame was now placed on alcohol consumption. Ignoring the warning signals he continued on his journey home. Back to nothing but loneliness.

In spite of the time constraints and the extra attention caused by the magazine article Abbey had bought herself some new clothes: a low-cut red dress, which would leave very little to the imagination and show off her long legs. It made her feel a little better, but she was still upset by the day's events: why should this happen to her again? She was so wrapped up in thought she didn't notice that a man had been following her for some time, at a safe distance.

Thick-set, dressed in a black overcoat, the man quickened his pace. Spying the alleyway ahead, he slowly pulled a knife from his pocket. He looked around. The street was deserted. He reached into his other pocket and pulled out a balaclava-ready to strike.

Abbey became aware of a figure moving swiftly towards her from the rear. She started to turn around. Too late!

The man pounced, grabbing Abbey from behind covering her mouth to stop her scream. She struggled furiously, but the grip restricted her movement. He thrust the knife towards her eyes. She was petrified.

"Don't even think about screaming. I'll stab you in the eyes and fucking blind you, bitch! Get up the alley!"

She slipped, the knife nearly embedding in her left eye.

"I said not to try anything! I'm not afraid to use this!"

Abbey gave up the struggle; with any luck he would take her money and leave her alone. The man shoved her violently up the alley and she fell against the wall. She started sobbing. He turned her towards him. She was now face to face with her attacker.

"I know you-you're that actress." His eyes surveying her from top to bottom, he licked his lips. "Give me your money."

She scrambled for her purse, ripping out the roll of notes and thrusting them in his face. He slowly removed them from her hand, rubbing it gently before tucking the money in his pocket. Abbey shivered, horrified by the thought of him touching her.

"Good girl," he yelled menacingly. "Now face the fucking wall… now!"

Abbey obliged, petrified by the ordeal. He grabbed her, and using the knife to rip her coat, he grabbed her breast, squeezing it tightly. Abbey was now inconsolable.

"Please don't," she pleaded, tears streaming down her face. "I gave you what you wanted – my money."

He ignored her, continuing to squeeze her breast. He put the knife in his pocket and moved his free hand down to her legs, forcing them apart. Abbey was thrown off balance, toppling her and the attacker to the floor. One of his hands was crushed against the hard pavement, causing him to release his grip on her. She spun round forcing her knee into his groin. He recoiled in pain towards the alley exit, blocking her escape route. She screamed in desperation at the top of her voice, praying someone would hear and come to her assistance.

A scream… someone in trouble… where?… yes, it was coming from the alleyway ahead. Matt raced towards the entrance.

"You're gonna pay for that bitch!" the man growled, holding his groin whilst taking deep breaths to relieve the pain.

Abbey was hysterical, tears streaming down her cheek. "Let me go!" The shriek gave way to loud sobs.

He threw himself forward, against her, knocking her off her feet and climbing on top of her. He slapped her hard across the face, drawing blood from her lip and reached into his pocket for the knife. Abbey closed her eyes: this was it; he was going to kill her.

3

As Matt reached the alleyway, he saw the attacker pressing Abbey to the floor.

"Get off her!" he yelled.

Abbey's eyes sprung open. She stared past the attacker at Matt, her eyes pleading for help. She looked up at her attacker. He was grinning.

"You stay put; I'll be back for you in a minute." His eyes were wide with excitement. Abbey tried to move but, instilled with fear, she remained motionless.

"You should've kept your nose out of this, punk," he growled. "For that, I'm gonna carve you up good!"

He raised his knife, motioning that he would cut Matt's throat. Matt took a step back, but he did not dare run. The attacker would either catch him or harm the girl. He lurched forward onto the attacker, knocking them both to the floor. He tried to get up but could not muster the strength. Dizziness struck. He fought it, straining every sinew in his body to rise to his feet. It was no use. They were both going to die. He stood there chuckling, watching Matt's attempts to get up. He then thrust his foot into Matt's abdomen, kicking him repeatedly. The pain so great, Matt yelled out in agony. He was close to blacking out, his strength fading away. Was he dying?

Suddenly there was a noise. A loud noise… What was it?… A police siren?… Yes of course it was, but would it be here in time?

The assailant spun around, planted one last kick into Matt's stomach and ran. The noise became more audible, now very close. A flashing light, tyres screeching, footsteps moving quicker, running. Someone was in pursuit of the attacker. There were numerous shouts. Had they caught the bastard?

Abbey started shaking uncontrollably. She had just faced the most frightening experience of her entire life. After a couple of failed attempts, she managed to stagger to her feet.

My God! Her rescuer! Was he all right? Just then, a figure appeared at the alleyway entrance. It was a policeman. Matt began to come too and could sense someone standing over him. *Focus, damn it!* He thought. Yes… a woman! She bent down. Something wet landed on his face: only small a tear, maybe, or blood.

"Thank you, you probably saved my life!" Abbey was holding back the tears. "Are you badly hurt?"

Seeing his face for the first time, she instantly recognised him: he was one of the bank staff from earlier, the autograph hunter. Matt was slowly becoming more coherent. "Don't think so! How about you, Abbey?" She was finally in focus.

“I’m fine, thanks to you,” Abbey replied, now perking up. “I was wondering when you would recognise me.”

“You look very pale. As white as a sheet!”

She knelt down, lifting his head, putting it into her lap. She began to stroke it gently. His eyes began to flicker. He looked dreadful. The colour had drained from his face. “I’ve been feeling very dizzy today. Oh God! I can’t feel my legs! I think I going to pass…”

The desperate tone vanished as Matt’s words trailed off. His world slowly descending into darkness, he lost consciousness. Abbey panicked. She shook him, but there was no reaction.

“God he’s passed out! Quick, call an ambulance!” Abbey screamed.

The policeman rushed over. “Is he still breathing?”

Abbey checked. He was.

“I haven’t a clue for how much longer,” she responded anxiously. “Get an ambulance, fast! I won’t let this man die, he saved my life.”

The ambulance arrived minutes later. Two paramedics emerged; one remained by the back door, awaiting instructions whilst the other knelt down beside Matt and Abbey.

“What happened?” Asked the paramedic.

Abbey recounted the events of the last few minutes, hurriedly, keeping a constant eye on Matt, as she explained that her attacker had kicked him repeatedly.

“He’s lost a lot of blood, by the look of him. We must get him to hospital fast. Does anyone know him?”

“No!” screamed Abbey. “Please help him! He saved my life!”

"He needs to get to hospital soon. Does anyone know his name?"

"No, he came from nowhere," Abbey replied. "I'll check his pockets."

Abbey frantically rummaged around in his pockets, searching for some clue as to Matt's identity. Finally she found his wallet, along with a CD, which must have been broken in the ensuing struggle.

"He's called Matthew, Matthew Preston!" She thrust a driver's licence in the policeman's face. The paramedic moved his face close to Matt's.

"Matthew, can you hear me?"

No response. Wait… there was a faint sound. Matt was delirious and drifting in and out of consciousness. "Have we a next of kin listed anywhere?"

"Yes, his mother," replied Abbey reading from his donor card.

"Well, I suggest we contact her. Get on the radio now!"

"I'm going with you," Abbey said. "He saved my life!"

The paramedic nodded. Abbey helped him lift Matt onto the stretcher and grabbed his hand.

"Please pull through, Matthew," Abbey whispered in his ear.

This was all my fault, she thought. As a result of his willingness to protect her, he could die.

The paramedic climbed in the back with Matt and Abbey. He immediately inserted a drip into Matt's arm.

"That should help him. Quick, radio ahead to the hospital so they can be ready for us. He's touch and go."

Abbey looked up at the paramedic in horror, then back down at Matt. She started to cry.

"It's all my fault!"

Norma Preston sat in her favourite armchair thoroughly bored. Tonight usually consisted of a trip to the bingo hall. Unfortunately, her accomplice was unwell and Norma hated going solo. Since the untimely death of her husband she craved an active lifestyle. Being cooped up in the house meant reliving painful memories of her husband's illness.

She leaned over to the coffee table with a sigh and grabbed the TV remote to change channels. After a few minutes of channel-hopping she turned it off.

"Rubbish on again!" She murmured.

Norma slumped back into the chair. What could she do? Housework? Up to date! Ironing? Finished this afternoon!

"Oh, Phillip, life's not the same! I do miss you."

The knock was hurried, persistent. Norma rushed to the door: she could see an outline of a police officer. *What now?* she thought, whilst reaching for the door latch. She opened the door.

"What's the problem, officer?"

"Mrs Preston, can I come in please? It's about your son…"

The policeman quickly informed her of the night's events: she was horrified. She dashed upstairs to get her coat and shoes, and they raced off to the hospital.

The relatively brief journey appeared to last an eternity for Abbey. She felt like a spare wheel. The paramedic advised her to continuously talk to Matt but nothing came to mind. It wasn't as if she knew him and could recall happy events.

"I'm really sorry. I just don't know what to say!"

He touched her arm as an act of reassurance, "Don't worry, miss! You've had quite an ordeal too! I'll talk, you just hold his hand!"

Abbey stared at Matt. He would repeatedly drift in and out of consciousness; his eyeballs kept rolling upwards underneath his eyelids, making him look like a character from a horror film. The whites of his eyes were prominent.

The ambulance arrived, greeted by a doctor and three nurses who watched the paramedics lift Matt onto the trolley provided. One of the paramedics relayed his findings as they sped through the entrance towards an examination room with Abbey in close attendance.

"Mr Preston was involved in an attack helping this young lady. No external injuries. He's drifting in and out of consciousness, but stable."

A nurse moved closer to Abbey, endeavouring to examine her only to be encountered with considerable resistance.

"I'm fine, honestly!" she stated, glancing past the nurse in an attempt to maintain her view of Matt's whereabouts. He was entering a free room.

"Nevertheless, it's better to be safe than sorry." the nurse stated assertively as she led Abbey into a free cubicle. "Someone will be with you shortly."

She was true to her word. In a matter of minutes a female doctor entered from behind the curtain and closed it behind her. She gave Abbey a quick once over and was satisfied that she had no serious damage and sent her back out into the waiting area. She spotted the room where Matt was currently being examined and strode over in an attempt to enter. One of the nurses grabbed Abbey, preventing her from doing so.

"I'm sorry, dear, you can't go in there. The doctors have to check him out. We'll tell you any details when we know more."

All she could do now was wait.

"He's losing a hell of a lot of blood from somewhere. We are going to have to open him up quickly."

The consultant pressed on Matt's stomach: there was no reaction from him.

"I doubt it's a result of the beating Nurse. Has the patient's mother arrived yet?"

"She's on her way! The police radioed an ETA of about twenty-five minutes."

"They'd better hurry; we need to open him up fast."

Anxious to discover if there was any news of Matt Abbey marched up to the reception desk and asked the flustered-looking middle-aged lady for an update. Abbey was quickly dismissed and told to let the doctors do their job and to sit back down. Dejectedly she followed orders.

All she could do now was wait!

After about twenty minutes, Matt's mum arrived and rushed to where Abbey was sitting.

The doctor arrived, holding a piece of paper.

"We don't know what's caused your son's condition. We are pretty certain that the attack had nothing to do with it, but we must operate fast."

He handed Matt's mother the form to sign, which she did. The doctor asked about any possible allergies that could affect the operation: Norma said she was not aware of any. The doctor rushed off, saying he would be in touch as soon as the operation had finished.

Abbey told her the full story of events. Norma began to cry and Abbey consoled her.

"I can't take this. I can't lose my son as well as my husband. What have I done to deserve this?"

Norma had seen her husband deteriorating some years earlier from cancer. She had nursed him every step of the way and could only think that she was about to lose her son too. It filled her with terror.

"Can I call anyone for you?" Abbey asked.

"No dear, Matt is the only family I've got left. You go if you like; if you leave a number, I will phone you when it's over."

"I couldn't possibly leave you on your own, and besides, I feel responsible for what's happened to him. I must just phone my friend to tell them what's happened and where I am."

The doctors attached Matt to a life-support system. There was a real sense of urgency. The surgeon opened him up, meticulously cutting down his stomach with the scalpel. He then peeled back the flesh and was able to view his insides.

"Nurse, suction please. There is so much blood, I cannot see properly."

The nurse obliged, clearing the problem area.

"Well, that's unusual. You don't see that often in men this age..." Triumphantly, the surgeon continued, "Look there, at the bowel. It's been strangulated and has started to ulcerate. It's Meckel's diverticulum. We need to cut away this loop and remove the damaged section of the bowel."

The surgeon carefully cut away the loop, removed the damaged section and stitched the remaining parts together. All that was left now was to staple up the original incision. Blood was furiously being pumped back into Matt. His colour started to return.

Talking... so many voices... I don't recognise them. Matt was coming round. *Pain... so much pain.* He yelled at the top of his voice. It was unbearable. *What is wrong?... Can't concentrate... so much pain.* He yelled again, this time constantly... he was in agony!

A nurse rushed over and put something in his hand.

"Press this button, it's a morphine drip; it helps ease the pain," the nurse explained.

It was no good. The pain mounting to intolerable levels made Matt continue to cry out. The nurse rushed over to a table, grabbed something and stuck it in Matt's arm. The screams stopped. He slowly closed his eyes and drifted back to sleep. His ordeal over.

4

It seemed like an eternity… waiting. It was 1.30 in the morning and they had been hanging around for two hours. Every time someone came along the corridor, they expected an answer, only to be bypassed by them. Finally, the surgeon approached them. Norma studied his facial expression for any signs of the news he was about to deliver. He was completely emotionless.

"Your son is fine, Mrs Preston." The surgeon reassured them. "He was suffering from a condition known as Meckel's diverticulum, which is caused by part of the umbilical cord rotting inside him, creating a loop. The loop then wraps around the bowel, causing internal bleeding. We have had to remove part of his bowel, but we caught it just in time. This was not a result of the attack but a defect from childhood. It is common in male children but extremely rare: only around 10% of adults will be affected. He will make a full recovery in due course."

Both Abbey and Norma breathed a sigh of relief.

"Can we see him now?" Norma asked.

"We have had to sedate him because of the pain, but I don't see why not."

Norma rose from her chair swiftly but the doctor put his hand on her shoulder to stop her. She sat back down baffled by his actions.

"He's currently on his way to Mary Ward. Give us a few minutes to get him settled in then a nurse will come and get you!"

"Thank you, Doctor."

He graciously smiled and headed back up the corridor and disappeared round the corner. Abbey noticed the change in Norma from the positive news about her son. She was more relaxed!

"I don't mean to pry but you said earlier about losing your son as well, what happened to your husband?" Abbey asked.

"I lost him to cancer just over three years ago!"

Norma gave a detailed account of the events leading up to his passing. He'd developed a cough that just wouldn't clear up so after a month visited the doctors only to be delivered a bombshell: lung cancer! Weeks of chemotherapy followed which appeared to help only to discover that the cancer had spread to the liver and kidneys. The prognosis was grim; he was given weeks to live.

He begged the doctors to allow him home to die. He wanted to be in familiar surroundings and not cooped up in a cancer ward. The doctors reluctantly agreed and arranged for regular visits by the Macmillan cancer nurses to help the family.

Remarkably, he defied the experts and lived for

another six months. There were a few scares along the way but he eventually passed away in his sleep. She told Abbey that Matt was devastated and needed counselling to help him grieve.

Considering the considerable stress she was under, Abbey thought Norma had aged well. Her auburn hair appeared to be natural, no hint of dye or grey, and her figure was still slender but curvy. She estimated that Norma was in her early forties, but in truth she would be fifty in two months. She obviously took good care of herself.

"That's enough about me, dear. How does my son know you? He never mentioned that his circle of friends included celebrities!"

"Oh, I don't really know him. We met for the first time today at the bank! I needed some money out and my cash card didn't work in the—"

The conversation was interrupted by a nurse who informed them that Matt had arrived in the ward and she could escort them there.

Norma and Abbey were led through to the ward to where Matt was sleeping. He looked so peaceful lying there. He was plugged into various machines to monitor his condition and had a tube stuck up his nose, presumably travelling to his stomach, which acted as a drain on the wound and flowing down into a bag beside the bed.

Abbey noticed a cigar-sized object on the bed close to Matt's right hand.

"What's that?" she asked, pointing directly at it.

"That's a morphine drip for pain relief." the nurse replied.

"Isn't that addictive?"

"The device regulates the dose and switches off for a time afterwards. We know what we are doing."

Abbey considered that the nurse was being condescending. She hadn't experienced a situation such as this before and in her acting career she'd never starred in hospital dramas. The nurse noticed that Abbey looked offended.

"I'm sorry if I appeared rude." She smiled, trying to defuse the situation. "We get that a lot and we tend to switch onto autopilot."

Abbey smiled, appreciating the apology, and turned to observe Matt. He remained sound asleep. Norma perched herself on a chair to the right of the bed and tenderly clasped his hand to hold it. Abbey settled down in the chair on the opposite side of the bed. She was desperate to thank her saviour and was prepared to wait as long as it took.

"Can I stay here tonight?" Abbey enquired. "I would like to be here when he wakes up."

"So would I," Norma said.

The doctor was extremely reluctant but after minutes of protestation and badgering agreed that they could stay. A room would be readied for them to sleep in meanwhile they stayed at his bedside.

Abbey and Norma had fallen asleep in the chairs on either side of the bed. The nurses covered them with blankets to keep them warm. Matt began to stir, groaning. Abbey heard a noise, opened her eyes and stood up to see Matt's eyes slowly open.

"Where am I?" he groaned. "Ouch, what the hell

is wrong with me? My gut feels like it's been pounded on."

"Here, press this, it will help."

Abbey handed him the morphine drip. It slipped from his grasp falling back on the bed. He fumbled about with a great deal of urgency to reclaim it without success. Abbey leaned over and retrieved it before handing it to him, cupping her hands around his to help secure the drip. He pressed it, giving him instant relief. She released her grip and returned to her seat.

"Thanks. Am I dead or just dreaming!" Matt laughed, pausing as another acute pain shot through his stomach.

"Do you remember what happened tonight?" Abbey asked.

"Everything, but why am I in here?"

"You've had a major operation, but you'll be fine." She touched his hand and stroked his face. "Thanks for coming to my rescue tonight."

Matt turned gingerly towards his mum, who had also awoken. She smiled.

"You like to put me through hell. I was so worried!" she said.

"Did they say what is wrong with me?"

"Heckel's something or other…" replied Norma.

"Meckel's diverticulum." Abbey corrected.

"Sounds bad! What does that mean?" he enquired.

"Some problem from childhood!" Norma yawned, fighting exhaustion.

"I'm sure that you will be told in the fullness of time." Abbey added before yawning as well.

"Why don't you both get some sleep? You must be exhausted; I'll be fine. What's the time, anyway?"

Norma checked her wristwatch. "2.37am!"

He rolled back over, grimacing, another shooting pain striking him in the stomach.

"You must take it easy or you'll open up the wound!" Norma snapped.

"Why don't you both go home?" he mumbled, trying to squeeze out words with pain attacking again.

Abbey looked at Norma to gauge her reaction. She appeared pleased to be dismissed. Abbey guessed that the vision of her son in his current condition was too distressing to handle.

"If you're sure I'll go then, see you tomorrow. Nice to meet you, Abbey. Maybe I'll see you again?"

"I'm sure you will – I'm staying in London for a few days, so I probably will pop in again to see Matthew," she replied.

"Matt, please. Matthew is when I've done something wrong!"

Norma gave Matt a kiss on the forehead and waved goodbye to Abbey.

"You can go too, you don't have to stay on my account."

"I'd rather stay. I'll only wake up my friend, Sonya by going home, so I'll stay. Unless you want me to go?"

Just then, the nurse came in and told Matt to rest. She told Abbey to go into a bedroom that had been prepared for her. She gave him a smile and left the room. *Even with a bruised face and ripped clothes, she still managed to look gorgeous,* Matt thought. He managed a smile before the onset of more pain and lay back in bed, quickly drifting back off to sleep.

The shriek of the alarm echoed around the room; an annoying, high-pitched bleep that could wake the dead. An arm reached over and viciously struck the snooze button, reverting the room back to tranquillity. After a few moments the duvet was hurled on the floor to reveal Bully's tall, slender frame. He sat bolt-upright, scratched his jet-black hair and rubbed both his eyes. After a short period of adjusting his pants, he made his way across the room to the toilet.

The next task was filling the kettle and making himself a coffee. This was his proper wake up call. Whilst waiting for it to boil, his next task was to switch on the TV. Bully was a real creature of habit. He followed the same daily routine rigidly. Up until a couple of months ago he would smoke now but an innocent remark by his son made him quit. One day after a farewell kiss, he told him that he always had stinky breath, not like his mummy. Bully may have overlooked the stinky-breath part, but the fact that Johnny said Sandra's breath didn't smell gave him the required determination to succeed in quitting. His chosen replacement became a bowl of cereal.

Bully rubbed his chin. It was time for his shave. As he prepared to apply the foam to his face he caught a glimpse of the reflection of the telly in the mirror. He instantly recognised the alleyway near to Terry's pub. He rushed over to the remote and turned up the volume. Apparently a nasty incident was averted when a passerby disturbed a man attacking a woman. As soon as a picture of Abbey appeared on screen Bully nearly fell over in shock.

I wonder if Matt is watching, he thought.

At the end of the broadcast, he grabbed the phone to see if Matt had seen the story too, only to notice the time on the clock.

"Shit its 7.30am. If I don't get a move on I'll be late!"

He threw down the phone and rushed back to the sink to carry on shaving.

Abbey woke up. It was 7.30am. She threw off the covers and headed off to the ward. Matt was asleep, so she decided to go back to Sonya's. She pulled out her purse, took out some change and phoned for a taxi.

The taxi pulled up outside Sonya's flat. Abbey paid the driver and thanked him. She took a deep breath and walked through the lobby. She wondered why people were staring, until she approached a mirror. Glancing at herself in passing, she stopped in her tracks, backed up and studied her appearance.

She'd forgotten that, during the struggle, her coat was torn by the knife. Her clothes were covered with dust from being hurled onto the floor; her blouse had a dark handprint on her left breast; her face was swollen around her mouth and had the traces of bruising developing. She looked a right mess, but at least she had a change of clothes. *Her clothes*! With all the excitement, she must have dropped the clothes she had bought. Damn it!

She carried on to the elevator. The door was starting to close, so she began to run. Luckily, someone saw her and pressed the open button. She entered and asked for the fourth floor. On the way up, the other woman in the lift, an elderly lady, kept running her eyes up and down Abbey, obviously wondering what she'd been up to. Abbey just smiled back to her, in no mood for an argument, and looked up at the lift counting the floors: two… three… four. The bell rung. The doors opened and Abbey started to walk along the corridor to Sonya's door. She rang the bell, heard footsteps running across the room and the door opened revealing Sonya. She looked horrified at the state of her friend. Abbey took a couple of steps forward, flung her arms around Sonya and burst into tears.

5

Bully arrived at the bank breathless. He ran for the majority of the journey to avoid being late. He knocked on the door and one of the girls trotted over to let him in.

"Evening Jim!" she sniggered.

"Is Julia on the warpath?" He asked, scanning the room for her authoritative figure waiting to pounce on his indiscretion.

She shook her head. "We've only just got in ourselves!"

Bully sprinted past her and proceeded on his way upstairs to find Matt. He was nowhere to be found. He checked his watch: 8.25am and time to set up his counter. On the way back down he passed Julia's office. She held the phone and looked deeply concerned. Glancing up she spotted Bully and motioned for him to wait. He obliged. She replaced the receiver and momentarily starred morosely at the desk before composing herself to relay the details of the call to him.

"That was Matt's mum; he's in hospital!"

Matt was awoken shortly after 9am by one of the

duty nurses, Sandra. She was a young girl with short blonde hair and a very pretty face. Quite rounded, she had a smile that lit up her whole face. She was very softly spoken and told Matt that he must try to sit upright. He was unable to move, all his strength gone. The more he tried the sharper the pain in his stomach. Sandra helped him by grabbing under his arms. He pressed his elbows into the bed. They seemed to sink into the mattress as it felt like he had a ten tonne weight on top of him. Finally, they succeeded. Matt was sitting upright.

"There, that wasn't so hard now was it?" Sandra said, smirking.

Matt gave her a filthy look and a sarcastic smile.

"Right then, let's give you a bed bath."

He smiled. This was the life. Being bathed by a woman, and a pretty one at that!

Back at Sonya's flat, having been unable to sleep satisfactorily, Abbey decided to get up. She'd had a shower, changed into jeans and T-shirt, and wrapped a towel around her wet hair. Her lip was throbbing.

She entered the lounge and Sonya brought her a mug of coffee. She was still in her nightie. Abbey presumed that she was working later, otherwise she would be immaculately groomed. Sonya's job required flexible hours depending on the availability of the interviewee.

They spent the next hour talking over the previous night's events, with frequent pauses when Abbey would cry. She was still very shaken. As Sonya comforted her and she stopped. She would recount some more and the process would repeat itself.

"Oh, by the way, the police brought round a bag of clothes, presumably the ones you bought yesterday."

Abbey nodded. "Where is it?"

"In the bedroom, I'll get it in a minute."

Sonya placed her empty mug on the floor, clapped her hands and leaned closer to Abbey.

"So tell me then, your knight in shining armour, dishy was he?"

"Is that all you think about, Son?"

She nodded.

"Nothing special. Nice face, I guess. He's going bald on top and I didn't pay much attention to his body. I was just glad he was there when he was!"

"So not in the class of Pat then?" Sonya sounded disappointed. "Still, you only go for rich and famous."

"For Christ's sake, girl, you make me out to be a man-eater! You're as bad as the papers. I'm not even contemplating another romance now. Anyway, Pat might still be interested."

Sonya shook her head in disbelief. Abbey was crazy. She went to the bedroom and fetched the bag that the police had dropped off. Abbey sipped her coffee, flinching as the heat passed over the cut on her lip. Sonya returned and threw the bag on the sofa. Abbey peered in the bag: what was that? It was the CD that she pulled out of Matt's pocket, 'Change of Season-Hall and Oates'. The least she could do was replace it for him, but there must be something else she could do to repay him.

Back at the hospital, Norma had arrived. She walked into the ward and sat down next to Matt's bed. He was looking better by the minute.

"Well your bravery has been on the news today, although you are a mystery man, as no one has released your identity. By the way, I called work and spoke to Jim, he'll pop in later."

Abbey dried her hair and attempted some breakfast – a couple of slices of dry toast – but she wasn't hungry.

"Sonya, what do you think I should do for this guy, to show my appreciation?"

"I can think of a few things, but I thought you said he wasn't that sexy!" Sonya giggled. "Besides, you don't want to give him the wrong impression, do you?"

"I'm being serious!" Abbey snapped.

"Why don't you take him out to dinner or something?"

"That's a good idea. I'll pop over to the hospital today – do you want to come?"

"I'll come and take a peak, he might be my type."

"Good, we'll stop off and buy him a replacement CD."

Norma sat in the canteen, eating lunch. She was not particularly hungry, but the doctor was examining Matt, so she decided to grab a bite. She glanced through the door and noticed Abbey and Sonya walking past. She got up and ran to the door.

"Hello," she called out to Abbey.

Abbey turned round, stopped, and smiled.

"Hello Norma." She glanced to Sonya. "This is Matt's mum, and Norma, this is Sonya."

They returned to the canteen and Norma explained what was happening.

"We can go back in a minute. The doctor should've

finished by then," Norma said. "Have the Press or anyone spoken to you yet? You're a hot news story today."

"No, but they don't know where I'm staying and I haven't checked my mobile. They've probably phoned my agent!"

Norma finished her sandwich. They left the canteen and made their way to the ward.

Matt was sitting up reading the paper when he glanced up and saw his visitors. He smiled.

"You didn't have to come back. I imagine you're very busy."

"He is quite dishy, Abbey." Sonya smiled; Matt blushed. "I'm Sonya, Abbey's best friend… well that's what she tells me anyway. I presume you're Matt?"

Matt blushed again. He recognised Sonya from the TV, interviewing numerous 'A-list' celebrities and not being intimidated. She dared to ask the awkward questions.

"Stop it, Son, you're embarrassing him! I came to bring your CD back. I'm afraid it got broken last night, so I got you a replacement."

"Have you listened to it?" Matt asked.

"No, I got it en route."

"You should. I'll tell you what, you can borrow it and send it back to me when you have."

"OK, but I won't send it, I'll give it back when I take you out to dinner."

"What?" Matt sounded startled. "What for?"

"A thank-you for helping me out. Is that OK?"

"If you insist. You don't have to."

"I insist," she replied forcefully. "I'll pop in before I go back and arrange something."

Matt nodded in resignation. *Why was she doing this?*

Abbey and Sonya said their goodbyes to Norma. Sonya bent over Matt and kissed him on the lips; Abbey pulled her away.

"Oh, by the way, if I'm interviewed, do you want me to mention you or would you rather remain anonymous?"

"Don't give them my full name, or where I am, please."

Abbey nodded, then lent over to Matt and kissed him on the lips. It seemed to last an eternity, much to Matt's delight! It was now Sonya's turn to pull Abbey away.

"An extra thank you. I'll pop in before I go." She giggled and winked towards Sonya. "Come on, you, let's go before you start hitting on that eighty year old over there!

The old man in the bed opposite looked over in anticipation. Sonya winked at him and fluttered her eyelids. He looked ecstatic: she had made his day!

"I'll be back for you later, sir!" she joked. "I'm going home for a cold shower!"

Abbey pulled Sonya towards the exit and waved goodbye before Sonya jokingly attempted to double back, walking straight into Abbey blocking her path.

Matt was smiling from ear to ear, oblivious to Sonya's shenanigans. *Abbey Jones just kissed me, wow!*

"She seems really nice," Norma added.

Matt didn't answer. All he could think of was Abbey kissing him. "What? Er, yes, she is."

6

Bully entered the hospital, searching for signs to direct him to the correct ward. Norma told him Matt was in Mary Ward. He stopped at the reception desk to ask the way. The receptionist pointed to the stairs at the end of the corridor and he nodded his appreciation as he started the walk along the corridor. Up ahead… no… It couldn't be!

As he reached the two ladies, he stopped. It all seemed surreal. Abbey Jones, the actress, had just been visiting his best friend along with another glamorous woman who also appeared on the television interviewing film stars. Matt's life had definitely altered since yesterday.

"Hello, remember me?" he enquired, gazing back and forth at them.

"How could I ever forget, the ID man?" Abbey giggled.

Sonya remained silent, staring at him. Bully noticed, momentarily distracting him, before refocusing his attention to Abbey.

"How is he?"

"He looks good considering; he said the pain is gradually easing. Look… about yesterday… I didn't mean to be quite so rude. I'd had a bad day."

"It's all right. Look, as much as I'd like to chat, I'd better get up there, otherwise he'll think I not coming."

The girls walked off to call for a cab.

"His mate's quite tasty!" Sonya observed.

Abbey glanced back in an attempt to gain a second look but could only see the back of his head. She didn't possess Sonya's eye for detail and, even though she'd seen Bully twice and Sonya had only glimpsed him for a matter of minutes, she was under no illusion that if they were asked to give a description separately Sonya's would be more accurate.

"If you say so."

Bully continued his walk to the ward. *The lucky bastard! She had come to visit him with another beauty.* Bully smiled. *Some guys have all the luck.*

Back in the ward, Matt listened to his mum talking about the news and the reporters being unable to contact Abbey or find out the identity of the mystery hero. The police would not reveal who it was; they would only say that he had been rushed to a hospital. Matt found it highly entertaining, finding it difficult not to laugh, but eventually he relented.

"Ow, stop it mum." The pain was intense. "It's agony when I laugh!"

Bully finally found the ward. He scanned the area looking for Matt's bed and found it at the end, next to the window. He waved, catching Norma's eyes; she waved him over. He had a broad smile on his face.

"You lucky bastard! Sorry, Norma, pardon my French. She came to visit you then?"

"She stayed all last night too!" Matt was gloating.

"Bas..." he trailed off, looking at Matt's mum, who was frowning, "Sorry, keep forgetting my manners."

Norma smiled. "Can't you complete a sentence without a swear word in it?"

Bully blushed, chuckling nervously.

"Tell me all about it then!"

As Sonya and Abbey reached the door, the phone rang; Sonya pulled her keys from her pocket, unlocked the door and ran to answer it.

"Hello... oh, it's only you... hold on. Abbey – it's Pat."

Sonya gave Abbey a disapproving look and held the phone out at arm's length. Abbey raced over to the phone snatching out of Sonya's grasp.

"I've just heard – are you OK?"

"Yes I am," Abbey replied. "I was..." The phone went dead. Abbey pressed the button to see if Pat had been cut off. He hadn't. He had hung up. She now knew that he did not care! She put the phone down and slumped down in the chair.

Sonya guessed what had happened from Abbey's reaction. She formed quick opinions of people and they were rarely flawed. Pat was an arsehole! Corrupted by money and fame.

"Why don't you come out with me tonight?" Sonya asked, "I'm going clubbing."

"I really don't feel like it," Abbey replied, "You go, I'll be fine."

Sonya left the room to pick out her outfit for the evening. Abbey sat slumped back on the sofa. Why was every man she dated a pig? Surely not everyone was like that, or were they? Did men have this built in ability to make women's lives a misery? Her father was the same. He constantly cheated on her mother, coming home smelling of perfume, demanding dinner then, going out again, only to return home in the early hours. Her mother eventually threw him out when Abbey was thirteen. She had not seen him since: eleven long years without contact.

The phone rang. Abbey reached over. "Pat?"

"No, sorry. This is Nigel Norfolk, reporter for a daily newspaper. Can I speak to Miss Jones, please?"

She knew the name instantly. A tenacious reporter with a tendency to bend the rules for a good story. A number of colleagues had crossed paths with him before and suffered.

"How did you get this number?"

"I have ways and means," he said confidently.

"What do you want? An interview?"

"Would you like to tell your side of events, like, who helped you?"

"He would like to remain anonymous. Besides, he's in hospital so you can't speak to him."

"Go on, you know I'll find him in the end."

"I said no!" Abbey slammed down the phone.

It rung again, she angrily picked it up. "Don't you people understand no?!"

"Abbey? It's Rita – how are you doing?" Rita was Abbey's agent. "How do you feel about appearing on the *Tony and Teresa Show*, to talk about the ordeal?"

"OK."

"Good. A car will pick you up at 9am and take you to the studio. See you, bye."

Matt was now feeling very tired. He could barely keep his eyes open, yet waves of acute pain kept him from falling asleep. Conversation between the three of them proved to be difficult with constant disruptions from doctors and nurses carrying out their observations. Bully conveyed everyone from works concern and best wishes for a speedy recovery. Over the coming days most of the staff stated intent to come and visit him.

"I think we should go now, Norma," Bully whispered. "He'll be asleep before long."

Norma kissed Matt on the head as they left. Bully offered her a lift home, but she had brought her car. They said their goodbyes and drove off.

Abbey was feeling miserable: dumped again. Sonya had gone out and she had started to drink copious amounts of wine. Two bottles later, she was drunk, and feeling even more miserable. She reached down for her glass and her hand was unsteady as she saw two of them. She knocked the glass over, spilling the contents across the coffee table. *Damn!* She staggered to the kitchen, swaying from side to side, bumping into the doorframe. Reaching for a cloth, she noticed the CD on the side. She picked it up and read the cover.

I will give it a listen, she thought, fumbling with the case. As she tried to open it, it sprung open. The disc flew out and bounced on the floor. She bent down to pick it up, but fell over, due to alcohol consumption. She giggled, attempted to recover it several times before finally succeeding. She put it in the machine and pressed play. Track 1: too rocky; she moved on. Track 2: boring. Track 3: not bad and so she listened to it fully. Track 4: awful. She was beginning to regret putting in on in the first place. Track 5: *wow, now this was more like it, a ballad*. The piano featured heavily; the voice, so soulful, hitting the high notes so effortlessly. It was if the singer had thrown everything into the song. She was hooked.

The rest of the album was as just as good. Abbey could feel the hairs on the back of her neck stand on end. She played it again. Her eyes welling up. She could feel the emotion of every song. The tears came. She picked up the phone, dialled Pat's mobile and got through to his answer service.

"I'm glad you dumped me, delighted in fact, because you treated me like dirt. Well, don't come running back – I'm not interested!" She slammed the phone down, knocking it of the table. Drink defeating her, she passed out.

Sonya turned the key in the lock and tiptoed in barefoot, expecting Abbey to be in bed. The lights were on; the phone was beeping and strewn across the floor. Abbey was lying on the sofa, snoring. Sonya went to the bedroom, pulled out a blanket from the drawer and wrapped it around Abbey. She stirred, briefly, and then continued to snore. Sonya chuckled and went to bed.

7

Matt awoke with a start. *Crash!* One of the nurses had knocked over a trolley of instruments. He had slept reasonably well, as the pain was now less frequent and acute. He was hardly using the morphine drip. Maybe he would be allowed home shortly.

"Have you seen this?" The old man in the bed opposite asked, pointing to the newspaper.

"What's the world coming to? A young lady could walk the streets in my day without being attacked."

Matt sat bolt-upright, receiving a sharp pain. He had moved too quickly. "May I see?" The man nodded. "I'm sorry, I can't get it."

The old man brought it over. The headline splashed across the page was 'SOAP STAR ATTACKED: MYSTERY MAN SAVES DAY'. The article told of the incident, but no one was able to ascertain the identity of the hero, and Miss Jones was unavailable for comment. The paper asked for any information about his identity... probably to hound him, Matt thought.

"Give the chap a medal, I say," the old man shouted. "Need more like him."

As Abbey arrived at the studio, she felt extremely fragile, so hungover. Photographers and reporters, trying to get that 'exclusive' comment for their employers, greeted her at the entrance. She dashed past them, revealing nothing. She reached the doors and was greeted by security, who immediately formed a barrier between her and the Press. Inside, the show's producer, Brian Bosworth, greeted her. He escorted her to makeup, introduced her to Tony and Teresa, and briefed her on the show's agenda.

Back in the ward the old man asked Matt if he minded if he switched on the television. He didn't. The morning news was on and the main story, unsurprisingly, was the attack on Abbey. The police had a male suspect in custody and were currently interviewing him but were unable to comment on whether or when he would be charged. The bulletin switched to another reporter at the scene of the attack who stopped bystanders to canvas opinion. The general consensus was the mystery saviour was a hero and more people should follow his lead to stop criminal activity. Abbey's agent was even briefly interviewed by phone. Everyone was desperate to find out his identity but there had been no one step forward to claim responsibility or to make a positive identification. Matt wondered how long would his anonymity last.

The news ended after a couple of minor stories that were glossed over because of the interest in Abbey's attack. The weather followed the news: cloudy with the odd sunny periods throughout the day. The programmes broke for an Advert Break before Matt heard a familiar theme tune:

"Not the *Tony and Teresa Show* again." Matt moaned to himself. He decided to continue reading the paper.

"On today's show, we have a soap star in the news, Abbey Jones. She will be talking about her recent terrifying ordeal, that's in around *ten* minutes, but first…"

Matt stopped reading. *Oh God! What would she say?* Ten minutes seemed like an eternity, but finally, the announcement:

"Our special guest today is Abbey Jones. Morning, Abbey," Tony said.

Abbey went on to describe the night's events in detail, leaving out nothing, except Matt's name: she did not let him down.

"Well, Abbey, you were extremely lucky to have Mr X there," Teresa added, "This has caused a sensation with the papers, who are desperate to find out his identity. Are you going to share it with us?"

Matt tensed up unsure as to what her response was going to be.

"He asked me to keep it a secret." Matt breathed a sigh of relief. "But I can reveal his first name: it's Matt. Hi, if you're watching. I've listened to the CD, it's superb. I'll pop in again before I return to work. Hope you're well."

"You heard it here, folks!" beamed Tony. "Thanks for being here, Abbey; we'll be back after the break."

Teresa thanked her for coming on the show and Abbey left the set. She was presented with a black coffee, requested earlier, as Brian came over to thank her and phoned for the car. Abbey thought about visiting Matt but decided against it as the reporters would now follow her every move.

Matt decided to continue to read the paper. He glanced up and saw Claire staring at him. She smiled and walked off; she had twigged. She left the ward, as it was her break, and she told the other nurse on duty she was going out to get some fresh air. She reached a payphone and dialled a number.

"I would like to speak to Nigel Norfolk."

"Speaking."

"I know the identity of Mr X. Is it worth anything?"

"If the information can be confirmed you will get £1,000. Who is this?"

"I would like to remain anonymous. I will arrange for someone to pick up the cash from you later. He is Matthew Preston and he's still in this hospital."

"It will need to be confirmed before payment is made! What's your number?"

"I'm in a payphone. I'll phone again in twenty minutes!"

Norfolk replaced the receiver and barged smugly into the editor's office, who was in a meeting with a photographer. He was perusing various photographs to be used. This uninvited visitor was a usual occurrence and he continued flicking through the photographs waiting for Norfolk to speak. He remained silent.

"One day you'll knock first before charging in!"

Still silence, Norfolk awaited his full attention.

"Speak," he snorted, "I've not got time for your games!"

He dropped the pictures on the desk and scowled at Norfolk, accepting defeat.

"Got a potential lead on the hero of the hour!" he announced triumphantly.

The news caused the editor to sit bolt-upright in his chair. He ushered the photographer out the room.

"How reliable?"

"I've just got to get Abbey Jones' number from her agent."

The editor rolled his eyes and pointed to the door, "What are you waiting for!"

Norfolk lent over the desk and grabbed the phone much to the annoyance of his boss and dialled a number.

"Rita, this is Nigel Norfolk. Be a dear and give me that number for Abbey Jones again, will you?"

He stretched across the desk once again to prise the pen that the editor was using out of his hand and scribbled the number down.

"Thanks. I owe you one."

He cut off the call and proceeded to dial the number given to him by Abbey's agent; it was her mobile. It rang. Abbey answered.

"Hello, who is it?"

"Nigel Norfolk. His name is Matthew Preston, isn't it?"

Abbey was shocked. "H-how did you find out? Who told you?"

He deduced that the information was correct by her reaction. He gave his editor the thumbs up.

"A very reliable source, it would seem. Goodbye."

"Go get the interview!" Bellowed the Editor.

Norfolk headed for the door and walked out before turning back to the editor, "By the way, I need a grand from petty cash."

The editor picked up a paperweight from his desk and threw it at Norfolk who quickly sidestepped and avoided the flying object which hurtled across the adjoining office and smashed a mug on a nearby table. He peered round from his hiding spot.

"See Jenny and she'll sort it out," He pointed to his secretary, who then cast back a disapproving look due to having another mug of hers destroyed. She got up and then appeared behind Norfolk. He nodded and turned towards the secretary trying to avoid laughing at her misfortune.

"Jenny, a female will phone in about fifteen minutes to speak to me. She is going to see if I am going to pay her, so I need—"

"£1,000 in an envelope. I heard that bit!" Jenny interrupted. "She's on the phone now, line two!"

He raced to the nearest phone and sorted out the arrangements for the money to be collected then returned to Jenny.

"Someone will collect the money; tell security downstairs to release the money once they hear the code word 'dosh.'" With that he grabbed his briefcase and left to snare his prey.

It was too late; the phone went dead. Matt would be furious. Abbey had to warn him. She hurriedly dialled the hospital.

"I need to speak to Matthew Preston in Mary ward. Please hurry!"

A delay; the line went quiet; eventually a click.

"I'm sorry; if you want to speak to Mr Preston you will have to ring through on the payphone. The number is 020 8456 1826. He's not allowed to get out of bed."

Abbey hung up, frantically dialling the new number. It was engaged. *Damn! Got to warn him.* She pressed redial, still engaged. What could she do to warn him? She tried again. At last, it was ringing. A nurse answered and said she would wheel the phone over to his bed, but it would take a few moments. The phone went dead, then a male voice answered: it was Matt.

"Matt, it's Abbey. Someone's told the papers."

"I know, I read it…"

"You don't understand," Abbey interrupted, "the papers have got your full name. You are just about to be swamped by the Press!"

8

Matt felt uneasy; every visitor could potentially be from the Press, pretending to visit a sick relative in the ward. *Damn it! Who told them?* Abbey was sure it was not Sonya. He was sure that Bully would not do it, so who did? It was driving him mad. Who? Why? It made no sense.

Just then, a nurse came into the ward and approached him.

"Excuse me, Mr Preston, there is a Nigel Norfolk here. He wants to know if he can speak with you; he says he's from the Press."

"Not now. Tell him no."

Just then, a bright light flickered from the doorway: it was a camera flash. Now they had his picture. The culprit turned and ran out of the hospital. Another man stood waiting. He was huge, at least six foot four and practically filling the width of the doorway. He walked in and approached the bed.

This must be Norfolk, Matt thought.

"Please, before you ask me to leave, that stunt had nothing to do with me or my paper. Obviously my source is greedy and has contacted other papers."

"How do I know that?" Matt asked, scowling.

"You're just going to have to trust me on that. Now can I have a few minutes of your time?"

"Why should I?" He snapped, "You'll only print what you want to anyway and start digging up my past because the story isn't interesting enough. Can't you just leave me alone?" Matt pleaded.

"Everyone loves a hero, Mr Preston, we are here to give people what they want," he said.

"I've heard that before. I don't need the publicity right now: I need to relax. I could have died, you know."

"We will pay handsomely." He smiled. "We just want your side of the story."

"If I refuse?"

"Then someone will probably go digging and produce a fabrication. OK, how much do you want?"

"I don't want money, just some peace."

"We'll donate it to charity if it makes any difference?"

Norfolk was extremely persistent. Matt didn't currently possess the strength both mentally and physically to lock horns with him whereas he suspected Norfolk could and was fully prepared to do so.

Matt sighed. "Go on then, what do you want to know?"

Nigel's face lit up; he had won again.

The interview lasted about half an hour. Nigel furiously scribbled down every scrap of detail, from the attack up until the operation. He seemed extremely interested in Abbey's visits and the amount of time she had spent with Matt.

"Look, if you were saved by someone who was then rushed to hospital, wouldn't you hang around and show gratitude?" Matt growled, furious at the insinuations.

"Yes, I would, but it would be a great end to the story: a romance,"

"It will never happen; she just wanted to show her gratitude, got it?" Matt was seething.

"OK, OK, I get the picture, no romance. Still a great story, though. I'll drop off a copy for you later so you can read it before everyone else. Now, can I take your picture for the article?"

"Just get on with it." Matt was resigned. "I just want you out of here!"

Norfolk left. Matt gave instructions to donate the money to cancer research. God knows how the article might finish up, but at least he could get some peace. Due to that incident, the hospital decided to post a couple of security guards outside the ward to discourage others from attempting to get in.

The rest of the day passed with no trouble. No one else attempted to get in to interview Matt. Norma came and stayed for a short while, as she was going to the theatre, and Bully stayed the majority of the evening. He told Matt that he was sorely missed and all the customers were talking about was the attack, and speculating whom the mystery hero was. Bully was in fits of laughter. He said that it was so hard not to tell them that he knew who it was. When Bully left the ward one of the nurses turned on the TV for the news.

They mentioned the attack again, but this time they ended with the news that, according to sources from a certain newspaper, they would reveal the identity of the mystery man tomorrow, and have a full interview with him. Matt felt extremely nervous at the prospect. Just then, a nurse entered the ward and handed Matt an envelope: the article!

He read it immediately; the thought of leaving it filled him with dread. What if it was pure fantasy? What would Abbey think? The article was extremely accurate, describing the events down to the very last detail. Norfolk had also done his homework. He knew the schools Matt had attended, the qualifications he'd gained, and even dug up an old cricket photograph. He had painted Matt as a true hero, 'Best of British', and all that. He finished with the disappointment that there would not be a romance, like most good stories. Matt was relieved: he could sleep easy tonight.

Abbey was woken by the sound of the telephone ringing; Sonya answered it. One of the soap's producers, Dan Majors, was calling.

"Why didn't you contact us, Abbey?" he seemed extremely annoyed. "Did you think we would never find out?"

"No, Dan, I've been exceptionally busy. I just haven't had time."

"We left it yesterday, but you should have phoned last night. We didn't know what to think." He was calming down. "What about this Matt? You know he's talked to the Press?"

"I didn't, no. What's he said?" Abbey was surprised.

"Relax, it's fine." He was reassuring, "Do you think he's a glory hunter?"

"No, I don't. He's not like that!"

"The paper's using a potential romantic angle – what will Pat have to say about that?"

"He's history. He dumped me hours before the attack."

"Tell you what, lie low for a few days. Shelve any plans to visit him, allow the hysteria to die down and then invite him up to the set for a few days, all expenses paid, of course. It will be fantastic PR for the show."

He was revelling in another one of his ideas.

"Just let me know when you've told him and I will send out an official statement from the show."

"OK, Dan, you're the boss!"

"Try to tie in your visit with your return, and then you can travel up together… God, I'm a genius!"

"I will, see you in a week."

She put the phone down. *Poor Matt, they're using him to gain viewers. God this business was sick,* she thought.

She entered the kitchen where Sonya was munching away on a slice of toast. She poured Abbey an orange juice and handed her the paper.

"God, Nigel Norfolk is a genius with words. He'll turn this into his own mini soap opera; the public will be begging for more." Sonya spoke out of admiration.

Abbey read the article. She was right. He was a creative genius. He had built Matt up to be a Superman, who had just rescued his Lois Lane. He was even trying to create a love story, making the public hunger for more. *Shame there would not be one.* God! He even had her at it!

All day the phone was ringing with editors asking for

interviews; reporters were knocking at the door, begging for interviews – it was a nightmare. If Abbey were to go out, she would be practically stalked by paparazzi. She was a prisoner in Sonya's apartment.

There was chaos outside the hospital. Dozens of reporters were camped outside the entrance, hoping for a glimpse of the hero of the hour. Eventually, one of the hospital executives came to address the masses. He was practically blinded by the constant flashes from cameras, and he was faced with an abundance of microphones and tape recorders being thrust into his face.

"Mr Preston is unavailable for comment: he is unable to leave his bed. He is progressing well, but he needs complete rest. He appreciates your concern and will speak to you when he is able to get out of bed, so I suggest that you all leave. Thank you."

This had some affect. Only the die-hard reporters remained in case the last report was false. The others phoned through to their respective employers to inform them that there was nothing to report and that they were moving on.

Inside, Matt was having the morphine drip removed. The pain now very rare and able to be controlled by pills instead. He was starting to regain his appetite, although he was still not allowed to eat. The tube in his nose was starting to irritate. Every time he swallowed, he felt his throat close up around it, making it very tender. It was a vicious circle: the more he thought about it the more he swallowed; the more he swallowed the worse his throat became.

Claire brought in the washbowl: it was time for his freshening up.

"I'm going to remove the dressing now, so we'll be able to see the wound. I'll also be able to assess how well it's healing."

She removed the bandage. The wound ran from the bottom of his ribcage to his trouser line and thirty-eight staples held it together. It looked remarkably good considering it was only forty-eight hours old.

"When can I get out of here?" Matt asked, wincing as Claire caught one of the staples.

"Probably about a week, depending on how well you recover. You will need to empty your bowels as well, to ensure everything is OK."

Claire dried Matt with the towel, carefully avoiding the staples.

"I read about you in the paper today. Quite the little hero, aren't we?"

Matt was not listening. *Another week*, he thought. *I'll go stir crazy in here!*

Abbey was becoming increasingly frustrated. Sonya had gone to work and she was left alone to brood. She had taken the phone off the hook and stopped answering the door. Shopping was considered but she would definitely be followed. Watching the television became an annoyance because every news update ran Matt's story. Abbey was utterly bored.

She decided to listen to Matt's CD again: it was becoming addictive. Abbey sang along with the majority of songs and knew most of the words by heart as she had listened to the CD so frequently. She wondered how Matt was doing. She thought about going to see him – it might cheer them both up. She suddenly realised Matt was creeping into her thoughts increasingly: why was that?

9

Abbey could not get Matt out of her head now – she was so confused. A week had passed since the attack and she had deliberately avoided the hospital on Dan's advice, and because she was unsure of her feelings. She talked it over with Sonya and felt that it was natural due to the circumstances. The feelings were out of gratitude and nothing else. How could Abbey be sure? This was messing up her head big time. She had phoned the hospital the day before and it seemed likely that Matt would come home today, so she could not put the visit off any longer.

Matt could finally see the light at the end of the tunnel. The last week had been torture: there were times when he had felt he was going mad, stuck in bed all day, attached to various pieces of equipment and no visits from Abbey. What was he thinking? She had shown her gratitude, why would she need to come back? Helping her did not carry any obligation, no matter how much he would have liked it to. If the last week had taught him anything, it was just how lonely he really was. Hospital was just like home: no one to lie with or to cuddle. It was only now that he had had the time to think about it. *Abbey, please visit today*, he prayed.

Around midday the surgeon came round to chat to Matt.

"It's possible that you will be discharged today, have you opened your bowels yet?"

"Yes, twice yesterday." Matt felt despondent; he would still be alone.

"Have you walked about yet?"

"No, I was only unplugged from the machinery this morning."

He glanced toward the door – he could not believe it! She had come.

"Abbey!" he yelled, unable to contain his excitement. "Great to see you again. Are the Press still hanging around?"

"A few of them." She gave him a hug. "You look so much better!"

She sat down on the bed, smiling at Matt.

"Right, walk over to the door and back, have a rest then walk a little further. Make sure you have rests." The surgeon was firm but friendly.

Matt got up unsteadily and paused; it was great to be out of bed. He tried to move but could not. It was as if he had forgotten how to walk. No matter how hard he tried, he could not raise his foot to start walking.

"This is not unusual after being off your feet for a prolonged period. Your muscles have wasted due to inactivity. Try sliding you feet."

Matt focused all his attention on moving a leg. The concentration was immense. *Move, damn it,* he ordered his legs. Yes! His left leg shuffled a matter of inches. The relief was obvious on his face. The right one did the same; he was moving. It was torture, but he had succeeded. The journey should have taken a couple of seconds but took practically five minutes. He looked like a frail elderly person, very slow and very uncertain on his feet. Abbey cupped her hand over her mouth in an attempt to mask her sniggering.

"How old are you, 100?" She burst out laughing.

"Twenty-seven, but I feel 100."

Matt gave Abbey a stern look. He was not pleased at the mockery. "It's bloody hard work! It's like learning to walk all over again."

"It will get easier. I'll pop back this afternoon to see how you are getting on. If you pick up your speed and appear steadier on your feet I will discharge you."

The surgeon left the room smiling. No matter how many times he saw instances like that it still made him laugh.

The doctor's words replayed repeatedly in Matt's mind. He was determined to get out. No matter what it took, he would do it.

Over the next couple of hours, Matt kept walking and resting. The effort was immense. He had sweat pouring down his face and the concentration was mentally exhausting, but he was building up his speed and the unsteadiness had gone.

Norma arrived an hour later. She looked quite distressed watching her son continually torturing himself trying to walk. Matt was ready for another go.

"I'll walk with you, now I can match your pace." Abbey smirked. She linked her arm with his. "Try not to pull me over."

She gazed into his eyes, "You have gorgeous eyes – a lovely colour and such long lashes. I would kill for those!"

Matt laughed, "I'll leave you them in my will!"

Abbey didn't respond, she was still gazing into his eyes with her head tilting slightly, "Er, sorry." She blushed and, feeling embarrassed, stared at the floor.

They walked the entire length of the ward, out into the corridor and back again. Matt was exhausted by now, but he felt confident as he slumped back onto his bed.

Abbey suddenly remembered her conversation with Dan.

"Oh, I nearly forgot, the show's producers have invited you up to Manchester to watch the filming for a week. They will pay all the costs, hotel, food, whatever you like. Would you like that?"

"Yes, it beats sitting at home watching the same videos over and over again." Matt tried hard to sound casual.

"Instead of staying in a hotel, stay with me: I've got a spare room. You can stay as long as you like and if you are released today, we can travel up on the train together tomorrow."

"I don't envy you: he's so untidy, take my word for it. I had twenty-two years of clearing up after him." Norma could not resist.

"Mum, don't embarrass me!" Matt gave Norma an evil look, "Anyway, I'm tidy now, you've said so yourself.

"Norma, do you fancy grabbing a bite to eat? 'Cos I'm starving."

She nodded and they got up and walked to the canteen, leaving Matt alone. He picked up a paper and started to read.

In the canteen, Norma and Abbey browsed through the food on display. "I think I'll have the prawns. What would you like, Norma?"

"I fancy the egg mayonnaise."

Abbey removed the sandwiches from the glass cabinet, paid the cashier and pointed out a spare table for them to eat. As they walked over to the table Norma offered Abbey money for the sandwich, but she refused it.

"Can I ask you a question, Abbey, a personal question?"

Abbey nodded, "'Course you can."

"Do you have feelings for my son?"

Abbey paused, shocked at the directness of the question. *Did she?*

"I honestly don't know. I mean, he protected me from an attacker. My feelings are all mixed up."

"All I ask is that you don't mess him about or lead him on, he's had enough previous girlfriends do that to him."

Abbey knew exactly how he felt: how many men had treated her the same?

"Don't worry, I wouldn't do anything like that."

They ate their sandwiches and made their way back to the ward without any further conversation. Abbey had been warned! As they entered the ward, they noticed that Matt had a smile on his face. He was listening to the doctor.

"You must take it easy. No driving, no lifting, just complete relaxation. You will need to be absent from work for at least six weeks."

"No problem, Doc. What about the staples? Because I'll be staying in Manchester for a week." Matt asked.

"They will need to be removed in a couple of days, let me know where you're staying and I'll get in touch with a local district nurse. Now get out of here. Remember: plenty of relaxation."

Abbey scribbled down her address then handed it to the surgeon. Matt drew the curtains around the bed, telling both Norma and Abbey to meet him in the corridor. He changed into blue tracksuit bottoms, white worn trainers and a white T-shirt that his mum had brought in. He stared at himself in a mirror: he was barely recognisable. He looked thinner, a lot thinner, and a beard replaced a normally clean-shaven face – that would have to go. Matt waved goodbye to all the patients and nurses, and joined the ladies in the corridor.

Abbey grabbed Matt by the arm and moved her lips to within touching distance of his ear and whispered, "You know I said that there were only a few reporters," she paused, "I lied!"

Matt's head shot round to face her. "You are joking!"

Abbey shook her head. "There's at least thirty. You've been portrayed as a hero, what do you expect?"

"I'm no hero, I just happened to be in the right place at the right time," he groaned. "I'm just an ordinary guy, I don't need this attention!"

"You aren't going to be able to sprint away from them, you've only just mastered a slow walking pace. Face it, you are going to have to talk to them," Abbey said, shrugging her shoulders.

Matt stared at her in disbelief. She was experienced at this sort of thing, he was not. She just smiled and squeezed his arm in reassurance, "You can do it, it's easy."

Matt was filled with dread. He stiffened up, which slowed down his pace. He could see the exit and wanted to turn back. Abbey could sense his uneasiness and squeezed his arm tighter. They reached the door and stepped through to the outside.

It was pandemonium! Constant camera flashes and reporters fighting for a front row spot blinded Matt and Abbey. Cameras and microphones were being thrust in front of their faces and various people were yelling Matt's name. *This was hell! How could people put up with this intrusion on a regular basis?*

"Mr Preston, how does it feel to be a hero?" a voice yelled from the crowd, but Matt could not tell to whom it belonged.

"I just did what anyone would do. Heroes win wars, save lives. I didn't do much except receive a good kicking."

"I think that he did save my life!" Abbey turned to face Matt, "You are a hero in my book, no matter what you say!"

Matt smiled at Abbey and turned to face the crowd.

"Now, if you please, ladies and gentlemen, I've just been discharged from hospital and would like to go home. Please respect my wishes, thank you."

They fought through the crowd to reach Norma's car

and drove through the crowds. Cameras were pressed against the windows to get as many pictures as possible.

The ordeal was over, for now, at least.

They arrived at Matt's flat after about ten minutes. Thankfully, there were no reporters waiting. The flat was located on the second floor. There was no lift, just a wooden, creaky staircase. The walls were in desperate need of a coat of paint: what was once white was now more a pale yellow. They reached the second floor, which consisted of only two flats, one being Matt's. He pulled out his key, and unlocked the door. Inside it was very small. There were only three rooms: the lounge, which was also the kitchen, the bathroom and the bedroom. Due to a lack of space, there was little furniture: two armchairs, one tall pine bookcase, containing DVDs, TV, DVD player and stereo, with speakers either side of it. The walls were painted a bright green and covered with concert programmes hung, inside transparent frames. *Quite quaint, but in need of a woman's touch*, Abbey thought. The kitchen consisted of a sink, fridge, cooker and a couple of wall units.

"Welcome to my humble abode. What do you think?" Matt grinned, "Not quite what you're used to, I expect."

Abbey joked, "It's fine, a little on the big side, but OK."

Matt gave her a sarcastic smile. "Sonya's OK about me staying tonight?"

Abbey nodded. Matt went into the bedroom and after a few minutes of crashing around, he appeared with a suitcase. He then entered the bathroom and had a shave; he was ready!

10

Norma dropped them outside the building that housed Sonya's apartment. Matt studied the building from top to bottom and his mouth dropped open; Abbey put a hand under his chin to shut it.

"Come on, let's go – Sonya's waiting!"

Abbey led Matt inside the building. The lobby was deserted. Abbey pointed towards the lift and immediately advanced towards it tugging Matt along with her. She pressed the up button and the door opened allowing them to enter. Inside she pressed the second floor button and the door closed and the lift started its assent.

Moments later the bell sounded and the doors opened, permitting them to leave. All that remained was a short walk down the corridor. Abbey escorted Matt to the door and knocked. Moments later the door opened and Sonya welcomed them inside.

"I hope you like Indian – I've got a take away for us!" Sonya reached over and kissed Matt. "You look a lot better than the last time I saw you. How are you feeling?"

"Good, thanks."

The food was delicious. Everything was consumed, along with a bottle of white wine. Sonya was an extremely generous host. Abbey offered to do the washing up and Sonya slouched on one of the sofas chatting to Matt.

"So, Matt, are you fit enough for a threesome?"

He nearly choked on a mouthful of wine. "Pardon?"

Sonya giggled. "Sorry, I'm such a tease!"

Abbey walked in from the kitchen, "What are you two talking about?"

"I nearly put Matt back in hospital. I asked him if he wanted a threesome!"

Abbey smiled. "I'm just going to get ready for bed. I feel quite tired."

Sonya quickly followed and returned first, wearing a long black silk nightie, held up by thin shoulder straps. She looked ravishing.

"Like it?" She asked whilst performing a twirl to allow Matt the complete picture.

Matt gulped, "V-v-very nice."

She smiled, nodding, acknowledging his appreciation. "Thank you."

It was Abbey's turn. She was wearing an old pale blue blouse; her gorgeous legs were completely uncovered. The buttons at the top of the blouse were undone, revealing some cleavage. Matt tried desperately to avoid blushing. He mopped his brow and the girls both laughed. He was alone with two extremely attractive women who were flaunting themselves. He sat forward to cover another potential embarrassment: he was aroused. They were teasing him.

Sonya sat herself on one side and Abbey on the other. How far were they prepared to go to tease? Suddenly Sonya lent against Matt's arm and kissed him on the cheek, "I'm off to bed, big boy, goodnight all."

She walked seductively into her bedroom. She glanced round and winked.

"Sorry to embarrass you, Matt. Sonya's a right tease." Abbey touched him on the arm. "Do you want to go to bed?"

Matt stared at Abbey. "Pardon?"

"I mean are you tired or would you like to talk some more?"

"Oh, I am rather tired. I think I'll go to bed. It's nearly midnight and the train is at twelve-twenty tomorrow." He gingerly pulled himself to his feet and wandered into his room. He removed his trousers, shoes and socks, and climbed into bed. Abbey sighed and traipsed off to her room.

Matt spent a couple of hours tossing and turning and could not get to sleep. He was thirsty, so he went to the kitchen for a drink of water.

"Noooo..." It was coming from Abbey's room. "Noooooo..." she screamed again. Matt moved as fast as he could to the room, picking up a saucepan on the way. He reached the door, lifted his weapon above his head ready to strike and charged into the room.

Abbey was sitting upright with her head in her hands. She was drenched in sweat and sobbing. Matt scanned the room, but no one was there. She must have had a nightmare.

"You OK?" Matt whispered.

His voice momentarily startled her. She jumped, looking in his direction; her eyes open wide from fright until she realised that it was Matt; the relief in her face was obvious. She began to relax.

"I had a nightmare about being attacked, it was terrible. He was going to kill me." The words spluttered out in between tears.

Abbey grabbed Matt, pulling him closer to the bed.

"Please stay with me… please. I'm so scared."

Matt nodded and climbed into bed. Abbey rested her head on his chest and he winced in pain – she had forgotten his wound. He lay on his side, wiped away Abbey's tears and repeatedly stroked her hair. He smiled: she had settled back to sleep. My God! He was in bed with Abbey Jones! Wow!

Hours later Abbey awoke. Matt had rolled over to the other end of the bed and was sleeping peacefully. She smiled. *He's so caring*, she thought. Maybe, just maybe, she had found someone who would treat her right, but did he feel the same?

Abbey left him in bed. She kissed him on the cheek and headed for the kitchen.

Sonya was already up and dressed. She was wearing a cream blouse and grey pinstripe trousers, part of a matching suit; the jacket was hanging on the back of chair. She was interviewing a major Hollywood star today for her magazine and was meeting her in the Savoy. She wanted to look the part.

"I called in on Matt this morning and he wasn't in his room," Sonya said, grabbing Abbey to pull her nearer. "Is there anything you want to tell me?"

Abbey just grinned.

"No, you didn't!" Sonya sounded shocked. "That's not usually your style!"

"Actually, I had a nightmare," Abbey conceded. She could never lie to Sonya for long, "He came in to see if I was OK and I asked him to stay, that's all."

Abbey sat down and poured herself a coffee; she looked puzzled.

"What's wrong, Abs?"

"Sonya?"

"Yes."

"What do you think about Matt?"

"Seems nice, but I don't know him that well."

"That's not what I meant!"

"He's not your type," Sonya replied, taking a mouthful of coffee, "he's not a celebrity, he's not rich and he's not outstandingly handsome."

Abbey sighed and took a deep breath, "What if I said those weren't necessities any more?"

"I would say you need to convince yourself and not me," Sonya twirled her mug. "But look how you've been treated in the past."

"Could a relationship work though, between two people from different social circles?"

"Love conquers all, the old cliché!" Sonya stared into Abbey's eyes. "I thought I saw a twinkle. You're growing up at last."

Abbey looked upset, "God, you're right! But does Matt feel the same about me?"

"He may suffer from the same syndrome. If so, you will have a hell of a job convincing him." Sonya finished her coffee and stood up, "I suggest you quiz him, subtlety, though!"

Sonya left the flat and made her way to her interview leaving Abbey alone in her thoughts. She needed to know. She would find out on the train.

Abbey crept back into the bedroom, leaned over the bed and gently nudged him.

"Matt," she whispered, "It's 8.30am, time to wake up."

She gradually lowered herself onto the bed so that her face was in close proximity to his and held her most seductive smile. She found it tempting to move in closer and kiss him, but she resisted.

His eyelids flickered, he opened his eyes and smiled. "Morning. You're a nice sight first thing, even without make up." He reached up to touch her face; she cupped her hand over his.

"Would you like any breakfast?"

"I'd love an orange juice," he answered as he sat up scratching the side of his head, "and some toast, please."

Abbey went to the kitchen; she poured his orange and toasted his bread. She was buttering it when he came in holding the paper; they were still front-page news. They sat next to each other reading the article while Matt munched away on his toast. Abbey would often stop reading and catch a fleeting glance of him and return to the article. On a few occasions he would notice and offer a courteous smile in return.

"Right, I'm going to take a shower." Abbey stood up walked over to the door, stopped, turned round and added, "Coming?"

Matt just smiled, he thought she was joking. Abbey

laughed to make out it was indeed a joke. She left the room and headed to the bathroom shaking her head. Once inside she shut the door and locked it, confident that Matt would not follow. Normally when she would shower the door was left open to allow her man inside to join her. In the vast majority of instances they'd come rushing in like bees around a honey pot.

She undressed and reached inside to turn on the shower. As soon as it reached the right temperature Abbey climbed in and began to wash, constantly thinking of her predicament. Abbey started to formulate a battle plan to extract the information from him. This is going to be harder than she thought but she needed to find out his feelings. The time on the train would provide the ideal opportunity.

11

Whilst Matt showered, Abbey ironed the clothes he'd left out on the bed. Typical man, clothes were thrown in a suitcase and creased up. Why couldn't they fold them up neatly, it would certainly half the workload. She replaced the white t-shirt and black jeans on the bed and headed off to her room to get dressed herself.

Abbey decided to raid Sonya's wardrobe again picking out a pair of faded ripped jeans and a white blouse. Matt popped his head through the door to thank her for ironing his clothes just as she took off her bathrobe, leaving her in only bra and knickers. She spun round, making no attempt to cover her exposed body, leaving Matt somewhat embarrassed. She smiled.

"Now, don't tell me you've never seen a woman in only her underwear before!"

Matt shook his head whilst attempting to slow down his breathing. No one as gorgeous as her, anyway.

"I… I'll leave you to get ready then," he stammered.

Abbey nodded as he removed his head from the

room to return to the lounge, closing the door behind him. Moments later he called through the door asking if she would like a cup of tea.

"Yes please. I'll be ready in a mo!"

Sure enough she appeared at the kitchen entrance looking fabulous, even in casual dress. Matt handed her a cup of tea and they returned to the lounge. Abbey phoned for a cab and arranged for it to pick them up outside at 11.50am. The cab would sound its horn three times to signal his arrival. They had half an hour to kill.

Abbey turned on the TV and they watched the end of the *Tony and Teresa show*, much to Matt's displeasure. Boredom raging, he got up and decided to look out the window to watch the world go by. He stood there watching people congregating in the street below and he realised who they were: reporters! Matt watched as the crowd multiplied whilst Abbey collected her belongings and packed them up in a small luggage case on wheels and dragged it out to the hallway and placed in next to Matt's. All of a sudden, three sharp beeps could be heard from below: the taxi had arrived. Matt looked at Abbey – they were ready to face the hoards again.

Dozens of reporters now gathered outside to see Abbey and Matt. How the hell did they find out they were here? The cameras clicked feverishly as they left the building. They clambered into the taxi and drove off to the station. Glancing back, they could see many of the reporters piling into taxis and news vans to pursue them.

At the station, all the fuss drew even more attention to them. People stopped to stare; all eyes were on Abbey and Matt. Luckily, the train was very quiet. They had purchased second-class tickets and the only other people in the carriage were a dozen businessmen, a little girl and her mother.

The girl was no older than five. She had a sweet face and a pink plaster cast on her left arm, and she kept staring over at them. Finally, after a couple of minutes she whispered something to her mother, who shook her head. The child left her seat, and although her mother grabbed her, she managed to wriggle free. She was heading straight for Matt and Abbey, with her mother in close pursuit.

"You're on the telly, aren't you?"

Abbey nodded.

"Can you write your name for me?" She handed Abbey a paper and pen.

"You'd like my autograph? OK, what's your name?"

"Rebecca."

Abbey signed the paper and handed it back to the girl who turned towards Matt.

"My mummy watches you too, she says you're funny." She gave the pen and paper to him.

He was extremely puzzled; had she mistaken him for a comedian? He wrote a message:

'To Rebecca

I'm not who you think I am. I'm not very famous, but if I ever become a star, this will be worth money as it is my first autograph.

Best wishes,

Love,

Matt Preston'.

He handed it back to the little girl, who gave it to

her Mum to read as they returned to their seats. She laughed and explained to her daughter that she had made a mistake. Rebecca looked sad and Matt wished he had told the girl the truth. He felt as if he had made her look foolish. She started to cry and her mother consoled her. He jumped out of his seat and strode over to where the girl and mother sat. He crouched down and tenderly touched the girls arm.

"Hey Rebecca, don't cry." He felt even worse now. "It's all right; I've got something to show you…" He delved deep into his pocket, pulled out a pound coin and placed it on the table. "This is a special coin. It's my lucky coin, and when I'm sad, or ill, I touch it and it makes me feel better." He picked it up and waved it in front of her face. "I want you to have it… take it."

"Really! Cor, Mummy, I have a magic coin!" She leaned over and kissed him.

"Thank you so much, sir." Rebecca's mum was close to tears. "She hasn't had much to smile about lately."

"My pleasure, now you get better soon!"

Matt returned to his seat looking pleased with himself. Abbey could barely hold back the tears. This man was a saint. She had never met anyone quite like Matt.

"That was fantastic, the way you cheered her up. How on earth do you do it?"

"It's easy. I love kids and don't like to see them upset. Nothing special with that, is there?"

"No, I guess not," Abbey responded, "I've just not seen people do it before."

Matt was amazed. Was her world really that different from his?

The train pulled away from the station slowly, gradually building speed. Their journey should only last a couple of hours.

During the first half of the journey, there was a distinct lack of conversation. Matt was still tired and had fallen asleep, initially on Abbey's shoulder. She lifted his head, put her arm around him and his head was now snuggled against her breast. Abbey was deep in thought. How could she broach the subject of her feelings with Matt? She decided to be cagey, see if he had reciprocal feelings before revealing hers. She needed to get inside his mind. If she succeeded, what would she find there?

Matt was awoken by the conductor asking for tickets. Abbey had them and handed them over. The little girl looked over and smiled; his gesture appeared to have worked.

"How long have I been asleep?" Matt sat back upright to face Abbey, who was in a trance.

"What?" Abbey looked at Matt; he had broken her train of thought. "About forty minutes."

Abbey hesitated, no, she must find out.

"Why don't you have a girlfriend?" Abbey blurted out.

Matt looked surprised, "I… er…" He composed himself, "Who says I don't?"

Abbey's heart sank. "I'm sorry, it's just that you've never mentioned her before."

"Actually, that's because there is no one."

"But why? You seem likeable." Abbey felt extremely awkward, "You're not gay, are you?"

Matt gave her an evil look. "No I am not!"

"I didn't mean to upset you; I just can't understand why someone like you is not dating."

"Why is the sea blue, the grass green? I don't know. Women either can't take me seriously or they look on me as a brother, or best friend."

Stage one completed: no one on the scene.

"I've got a question for you," Matt stated, "why do you date Pat Keane?"

"He dumped me last week."

"Sorry about that. Why him, anyway?"

"On the rebound from someone else and he asked me out."

"You didn't love him then?"

"I didn't say that."

This was not going to plan; Matt had turned the tables.

"I still have feelings for him. He used to treat me wonderfully."

"Why do you always date famous people?"

"Because they go to the same places I do and they ask me out. Simple." She had to try to regain the advantage. "No one else has ever asked me."

"And you would say yes, just like that?" he asked sceptically, "I don't think so."

"Why not?" Abbey had to know.

"Because ordinary people and celebrities don't mix; we come from different worlds and the two aren't compatible."

"So you're saying someone like you and someone like me couldn't date?"

"Exactly. I couldn't shower you with gifts, take you

on expensive holidays and you wouldn't want to sit in an average pub with some of the lowlifes I see."

"What about love conquering all?"

"It's all a pipe dream. Reality is not like that, except for a few isolated cases."

"Oh," she was close to admitting defeat, "I guess you're right."

"I've yet to see anything to change my mind," Matt seemed very confident, "Even people who find fame later seem to exchange ordinary partners for more glamorous ones."

"Being with a high-profile partner isn't all it's cracked up to be. In my experience they treat you like dirt, then dump you when you won't sleep with them."

"Maybe you should try a relationship with an ordinary guy!" Matt replied, laughing.

"I might just do that!" Abbey responded defiantly, hinting her intentions.

"I'll help you find one!" Matt continued to laugh.

God damn it! He was not taking the hint. Abbey shook her head while Matt continued to laugh. He would not let his guard down and open up. How the hell was she going to sort this out? Right now, the only thing she could think of doing was stripping off and telling him she loved him. Even then, he probably would not believe her. She was determined to wear him down, no matter how long it took. She had to make him see sense. This was one man who would treat her right; he was one in a million.

"Some woman must have really messed you up in the past to make you this cynical!"

"All women, not one in particular. Your species are a

law unto themselves. I don't think you understand each other, so what chance do us men have? We have to look like Brad Pitt to get a look in, so us ordinary guys are doomed before we start!"

"I happen to think differently. It's what's inside that counts; it's how they treat you, not how much money they've got or what they look like."

Matt did not look convinced. "I wish there were some ordinary girls like you about!"

Bingo, she thought. She had an opening, however small. She would have to convince Matt she was telling the truth.

12

The remainder of the journey was uneventful. Abbey decided to catch some shuteye to avoid more confrontation with Matt. His anger and bitterness was increasing by the second but Abbey could not understand why. He appeared to be resentful of celebrities and women – he must know some real bitches. The train slowed and an announcement followed, informing the passengers that they were arriving at Manchester. Matt tapped Abbey on the arm to wake her and she opened her eyes.

"Abbey, I'm sorry about earlier, I've just had some bad experiences with women. Actually, they've all been bad experiences, one way or another. It makes you feel that maybe there is no Miss Right out there."

"I understand." Abbey felt happier she was winning; he was opening up gradually.

"There is a Miss Right for you, you'll see." She wanted to say that he was looking at her right now and she would never do anything to betray him, but he was not ready yet.

The train stopped. Matt looked out of the window, surveying the area. "Can't see any reporters, thank goodness."

Abbey retrieved their luggage from the overhead racks, while Matt continued to peer out of the window. Abbey prodded him, gesturing with her head towards the exit. Matt followed.

Outside the station there was a white stretched limousine parked. The driver was leaning over the bonnet, cloth in hand, presumably wiping away some dust. He obviously took pride in keeping it clean: it sparkled and looked brand new.

He spotted them and smiled. "Good afternoon, Miss Jones. Mr Raymond insisted that you and your guest be taken home in style and I was only to happy to oblige."

"Thank you, Clive. To my house, please!"

Clive opened the back door and loaded their belongings in the boot; Matt jumped into the limo. The inside was vast: all cream leather interior, fitted with a drinks cabinet and a television set. He just sat there, gobsmacked. Abbey got in, saw Matt's face and laughed.

"How the other half live, eh!"

He did not respond; he just sat there, gazing.

The journey to Abbey's house took twenty minutes, during which time they had a couple of glasses of champagne and Matt smoked a giant cigar – much to Abbey's annoyance, so much so that she insisted that he stuck his head out of the window.

This is the life, Matt thought.

Abbey's house was secluded. It was situated on its

own down a private road. The perimeter of the grounds enveloped with a high brick wall, presumably for privacy. The entrance was protected by wrought iron gates, operated by remote.

The house was fantastic. The outside was modelled on the old Georgian style; the front lawn looked immaculate, with a long winding drive dividing it into two sections. It had a double garage and the windows were lead lined. This was a true celebrity's house.

Clive carried the bags to the door. He bid them both farewell and drove off, presumably back to the studio. Abbey pulled some keys from her jacket pocket and unlocked the door. She outstretched an arm, "Welcome to my humble abode."

Matt picked up the bags and entered, Abbey followed.

"Nice place you've got here, Abbey."

"I'll show you around later. Are you hungry?" she asked heading to what looked like the kitchen.

"Yes," said Matt, studying pictures on the wall, "This your mum?"

Abbey came back into the hall to see which picture he was referring to. "No, that's the show's creator, Lorna Summers. She gave me my first big break in a mini-series – *The Young and the Reckless*, do you remember it?"

"Vaguely… was that the one about the school kids who killed the teacher?" Matt was desperately trying to visualise the cast, "Who did you play?"

"The girl who was driving when the teacher was killed and who was eventually betrayed by the other girls before seeking revenge." Abbey recalled it as if it were yesterday, "That was eight years ago."

Matt vaguely remembered the girl, "I would have never said that was you – she had long, jet black hair and really thick eyebrows, with no gap between. She was really ugly!"

"It's amazing what a wig and makeup can do," Abbey laughed. "It can even turn a princess like me into an ugly duckling."

Matt pulled a face as if to say 'Here we go again'. "Anyway what's for lunch?"

Abbey entered the kitchen followed closely by Matt. Christ! It was as big as Matt's flat, a mass of electrical equipment: cooker, fridge, freezer, washing machine, tumble dryer, microwave, dishwasher and so on. Matt sat down at the table whilst Abbey rummaged through her cupboards.

"Do you like tuna?" she asked, pulling a tin from the cupboard.

"That'll be fine."

Abbey went to her cutlery drawer and finally laid her hands on the tin opener. She carefully opened the tin and drained off the excess oil.

"Can you pass me the vinegar and pepper? They're in the last cupboard on the left."

Matt nodded, rose from the chair and sauntered over to the cupboard, pulling the condiments out. He walked over to hand them to Abbey, and as she reached out, she clutched Matt's hands softly and their eyes met. Abbey smiled, gently prising the vinegar and pepper from his fingers. Her hands felt so soft, as if silk had brushed down Matt's hands. He held his breath briefly, and then let out the excess air: her touch was so gentle.

"How many sandwiches would you like?"

"Er, um, er, two please." He was flustered.

After lunch the phone rang – it was the local district nurse. She arranged to come over on Friday morning to remove the staples that were becoming a constant irritation, catching on Matt's clothing and making the skin extremely sore. Matt could not wait for them to go.

They sat down in the lounge, Matt sitting in the armchair and Abbey lying on the sofa.

"What do you want to do?" Abbey asked.

"I don't mind, whatever."

"Let's talk then!" Abbey was on another information-gathering session. "What did you want to be when you were a kid?"

"A cricketer. Could have been one too with a bit better luck."

"What happened?"

"I was playing for the England Schoolboys' team, against Australia, when it happened: I was having the game of my life, batting at the time of the accident." Matt remembered it as if it was yesterday; his voice was tinged with sadness, "I was 121 not out when their fastest bowler landed the ball on a crack on the surface and the ball flew up and shattered my elbow, effectively finishing my career before it started."

"That's so sad, having your dreams shattered by a freak injury." Abbey really felt for him. "Do you know what I wanted to be? A nurse!"

"Why didn't you then?"

"Because of the long hours and poor pay. So, I got

into acting and never looked back." Abbey felt justifiably proud of herself, "Have you any other goals in life?"

"I take it one day at a time. I have no dreams; I just want to be ordinary. Anyway, I'm one of life's losers: everything I do goes wrong!" Matt sounded extremely sorry for himself. Abbey was fascinated at how a person could feel like that. Matt was riddled with self-doubt and seemed to have a complete lack of confidence. She was determined to help him, as he helped her – everyone had a talent for something.

Matt sat feeling totally depressed. Their chat had opened up old wounds and many unhappy memories. At this rate, Abbey would send him to a hotel and find ways of avoiding him.

Snap out of it you idiot, he thought.

"Are there any good pubs to go to? One that has live music or a good jukebox. That plays real music. Not all this modern crap. But 60's, 70,s and 80's music?" Matt asked, trying to sound more positive.

"I know just the place, you'll love it. I know the owner so we'll get the five-star treatment!

Abbey spent the next few hours planning their evening. They would go alone, giving her more time to work on him. She would get a couple of drinks down him and see what happened. They did not have to be at the studio until 2pm in the afternoon.

Matt asked to borrow an iron. Abbey offered to do it for him but he insisted. He decided to wear the grey silk, short-sleeved shirt that he liked so much, and his black trousers. He checked that they were suitable and Abbey approved, so he ran the iron over them as they had become creased when he chucked everything in the case.

Abbey had an idea. She called for Matt to come upstairs and help her choose her clothes; hopefully he would choose something sexy. Matt entered and Abbey laid various garments on the bed. She held each one up to give him an idea of how it would look. He had taste. He picked out her favourite dress, the red one. It was short, a couple of inches above the knee, not too revealing, but exposed her shoulders. This dress was a male magnet.

"With or without stockings?"

"With!" Matt was extremely aroused. This was unheard of: a woman asking his opinion about clothes.

"Right, it's 4.30pm, so we should be out by seven. We'll have a bite to eat first then have some fun and continue getting to know one another better." Abbey was pleased with herself – her plan had the desired effect. With time to spare, Abbey laid in the bath mapping out various courses of action. She had to be ready and have contingency plans; she decided not to rush things, just keep chipping away at his defences until he was hooked. It could take days, it could take months, it might never happen. No! Never is not an option; she would not accept failure.

God! I wish I could have him now, she thought.

Matt stood downstairs by her CD rack, flicking through the CDs to gauge her musical taste.

Apparently very little, he chuckled, but at least she seemed to like '60s music. There were a few compilations scattered around, some '80s, but mostly current music, club anthems, which were not Matt's cup of tea. And then there was *Barry Manilow's Greatest Hits*. Barry

Manilow! This was completely different from the rest of her collection.

He heard a noise: Abbey's footsteps on the stairs. She called his name and he spun round. She stood there on the bottom step, arms spread wide, awaiting Matt's approval. He gulped; his mouth fell open. She looked incredible, like a goddess. The dress looked a million times better with her in it and it hugged every curve of her body. He'd never seen anything as beautiful as this object facing him, with her lips painted bright red and her blonde hair hanging off her face, she looked perfect, just perfect. Matt felt an enormous amount of pride at the thought that he would be seen out with such a beautiful object. This was every man's fantasy.

Matt finally attempted to speak, "W-w-wow!" He cleared his throat. "I've never seen anyone look as stunning as you do now. I'm not worthy."

Abbey beamed. "That's one of the nicest things anyone has said to me! Thank you, you look good too!"

"I'm not in the same league. I should walk about ten feet behind you."

"Nonsense, don't you dare!" Abbey snapped back. "You will be the perfect chaperone."

What was Abbey up to? Was she expecting to see Pat and trying to make him jealous hoping he would take her back? That must be it – she couldn't possibly be trying to woo him. Maybe it was pity, or because he helped her. *Stop it, who cares, just enjoy spending time with this beauty.*

"I've called a taxi, it'll be here in a minute, and then I'll show you the good life."

The driver sounded the horn and Abbey and Matt

came running out of the house. He took them to the centre of town and it was packed. Everybody appeared to be out enjoying themselves. Abbey led Matt through the crowds, holding his hand tightly. This was quite normal for Matt, living in London. He was pretty used to it. The only thing that seemed strange was the constant stares from people seeing an actress walk past them with an unknown male.

They reached the pub, The Good Intent, which was reasonably quiet, unlike most of the others that night. This was an exclusive establishment, frequented only by celebrities, as it was membership-only and maintained high prices. They reached the bar, and an older gentleman, presumably the manager, smiled.

"Good to see you back again, Abbey. I see you've brought your knight in shining armour with you. Nice to meet you, I'm Albert and you must be Matt." He extended his hand out to Matt and shook his hand.

"Nice to meet you too, Albert."

"Whatever you want tonight is on the house, food included. I'm so glad you helped my granddaughter. I'm forever in your debt."

"Your granddaughter?" Matt was shocked, that he was not expecting.

"What would you like to drink, Matt?" Albert asked.

"Pint of lager, please."

Albert laughed. "'Fraid there is no call for pints of lager here. The clientele prefer bottles; they think it's more sophisticated."

"That's fine, but does it mean you don't sell burgers and chips, just caviar?" It was Matt's turn to laugh.

"Like it, a man who is laughed at and still has the bottle to fight back. No, we sell everything. I'd recommend the steak."

"Not the mushy peas, pie and mash?"

"Now you're taking the piss." Albert laughed. "Go on, sit down and I'll bring the menu over."

Abbey led him over to the corner. Each table had dividers between, allowing for privacy. She sat down and Matt sat opposite, while Albert brought the menu and drinks over.

The food was fantastic. They started with a shared dish of king prawns, covered with seafood cocktail (the chef's own recipe), followed by a rare steak for Matt and a pasta dish for Abbey. The drink flowed freely. There was very little conversation during the meal, just comments on the excellence of the food. Matt could barely take his eyes off Abbey, admiring her beauty, while she was concentrating on her plans for the rest of the evening. She looked at Matt. She obviously captivated him but would her lifestyle frighten him off, as he intimated on the train journey?

"Something's been bugging me," Matt smiled, "Barry Manilow?"

"My mum's a fanatic," Abbey laughed. "It was practically the only music I grew up with; besides, he has made some fantastic songs."

Matt nodded in agreement, "What's your favourite?"

"'Mandy'. I think it's one of the greatest ballads ever!"

"It's good," Matt nodded in appreciation. "Changing the subject, where are you taking me afterwards?" he asked.

"Upstairs," she pointed to the ceiling. "Granddad has

a party night for one and all. The DJ plays '60s through to present music, but he plays pop and disco as opposed to dance music. It's a sort of singles' club."

It sounded great. It had been a long time since Matt had been to this sort of function and, with copious amounts of drink inside him, he felt up for a boogie.

"Let's get up there!"

"Are you sure, in your condition?"

"I've only had a few!"

"That's not what I meant."

The drink had obviously affected his thinking, thought Abbey. Before she could do or say anything he was halfway up the stairs so she followed him. Who was she to argue if he felt up to it? Maybe the party would provide the perfect setting for her to make her move.

Albert waved and told them to come back down once it had finished. It was now 10pm, and the party was starting to liven up. The dance floor was crowded and the music was blaring from the speakers, which caused the room to pulsate. The sight of Abbey caused many heads to turn and the room seemed to come to a momentary standstill. The music drowned out the sound of heavy breathing, as the women glared at their men in anger. Abbey turned towards Matt and shrugged her shoulders, grabbed his hand and dragged him onto the dance floor. He felt compelled to comply, resistance was useless anyway. Matt was normally very self-conscious when dancing, even though he was a reasonable mover, but the drink removed his inhibitions. Abbey was poetry in motion; she commanded the dance floor and she knew it. Gradually she collected a crowd of men around her, preparing themselves to chance their arm, but they were about to be disappointed. She pulled Matt closer, dancing around him seductively and their faces dropped one by one. *Why him?* He looked like the cat that got the cream: he had.

The atmosphere was vibrant. Everyone was having a wonderful time dancing to the different decades, especially Matt and Abbey, who stayed on the dance floor for the majority on the night. By now, they were both dripping with sweat, which only served to enhance Abbey's beauty.

She would still look exceptional covered in mud, Matt thought.

"We've almost come to the end of the evening," the DJ informed the crowd. "This will be the last dance, one for all you lovers out there."

The smooching song, the one for couples to get close. Matt, who was used to sitting down for these moments, started to leave the dance floor.

Abbey grabbed his arm to stop him "I hope you weren't thinking of leaving without giving me the last dance," she yelled in his ear.

Matt shook his head, scarcely believing that he was about to snuggle up to the most beautiful women in the room. He glanced around to see many envious faces staring at him. He wrapped his arms around her waist, resting his hands just above her bottom. Abbey draped her arms over his shoulders, and nestled her head into his neck. She tightened her grip, pressing their bodies tightly against each other.

Abbey adjusted her head so her mouth was close

to Matt's ear, "I think I'm falling in love with you," she whispered, praying he would hear and kiss her.

Unfortunately, he did not as the music drowned out her voice, "What did you say?"

"I said I love this tune," Abbey yelled, losing her courage.

"Me too."

Why didn't I say it louder? she cursed herself. He's not ready yet, she thought, justifying her actions.

The song finished, the lights came on, and people said their goodbyes, leaving separately; some of the lucky ones left with new partners. Abbey still held Matt tightly, wishing the music was still playing, but finally had to let go.

"I 'spose we'd better go and say goodbye to Granddad," a trace of dejection in her voice. "Did you enjoy yourself tonight?"

"It was excellent. Thank you, Abbey," Matt replied, "Haven't had this much fun for ages."

Just then, Albert appeared at the door. "I've taken the trouble of ordering you a taxi," he called across the room, "He's down stairs now."

They said their goodbyes, walked back down the stairs and climbed into the taxi. Abbey gave the driver the address and he pulled away. They both sat on the back seat and Abbey laid her head on Matt's shoulder. He put his arm round her and smiled. Suddenly, he received a sharp pain in his stomach, jolting him forward. Another one hit him, twice as severe as the last. It felt as if someone was repeatedly stabbing him.

"Jesus Christ! The pain!" he yelled. "Help me, Abbey.

Get me to hospital, fast!" He was now doubled up in extreme agony. Abbey panicked, but managed to tell the driver to get them to hospital. Matt was clutching his stomach, his face contorted through pain.

"We'll be there in minutes, Matt, hang on!"

What the hell was going on? She asked the driver to go faster. She looked at Matt: he was still desperately clutching his stomach. How serious was it? The answers lay at the hospital.

13

Abbey sat patiently in the waiting room. Matt had been whisked away on arrival. After about half an hour, there had still been no contact. *Jesus! This was agony*. Should she phone his mum or wait? What was the time? 1.30am. She thought that it would be better to wait.

The door opened and in walked the doctor.

"Miss Jones?"

"Yes," she replied nervously. "Is it serious?"

"He's been lucky and very stupid!"

"What do you mean?" She was puzzled.

"He's supposed to rest and not over do things, so what do you both do? Spend the night dancing!" The doctor was not very impressed. "He could have opened his wound up again. Thankfully he didn't."

Abbey breathed a sigh of relief. "What was the cause of the pain?"

"Overexertion of muscles recently under-used, and the stretching of the wound that is still extremely weak.

He's had a pain-killing injection, but he must rest. Any repeat of tonight could kill him!"

"Can I see him now?" The doctor's words repeating inside her head had had the desired effect.

"You can do more than that, you can take him home." The doctor smiled. "Just remember my warning, I've already told him."

Abbey thanked the doctor and wandered out of the room to find Matt sitting in the corridor, looking very sheepish. She smiled. "Sorry, Matt, I didn't think the dancing could do any damage." She sounded upset and her eyes filled with tears. "I was very worried you would need another operation."

"It's not your fault. I should have been more careful and a little less drunk!" He warily rose to his feet and Abbey stood beside him, putting her arm around his waist to act as a support. They walked towards the entrance.

As they reached the door two men approached them. One pulled out a camera and took a picture of them, lighting up the night sky with the flash.

"Is it true that you started a fight tonight outside the party and that's why you're here?" asked the reporter, thrusting a small tape recorder into their faces.

"Where do you get your information from?" Matt was fuming. The reporter remained silent. "Whoever told you that is talking crap. Now piss off and find a proper story!"

Matt shoved the reporter out of his way. The cameraman captured the moment with another photograph as Matt attempted to grab the camera. He felt a quick shooting pain. He was overexerting himself again.

"You're not worth it!" He turned his back and walked towards a taxi that was just pulling up outside the entrance, leaving Abbey to face them.

"Your information is wrong," Abbey stated. "Matt had no punch up, he just danced too much."

She left to join Matt and they jumped into the taxi, gazing backwards to witness a multitude of sparkles that were obviously the flashes on the camera. Abbey grasped his hand in hers and repeatedly enquired if he was in pain on each occasion that she noticed him flinch and touch his stomach, much to Matt's annoyance.

He sensed another enquiry coming. "Yes, I'm still OK!" he barked.

"I wasn't going to ask!" she replied. "All I was going to say was I hope there's no repercussions after tonight!"

"As long as I take it easy."

Abbey shook her head. "Not your injury, the reporters!"

Matt didn't understand what she meant but couldn't be bothered in his current state to question her. He just nodded and smiled.

Once they were back at her house, Abbey unlocked the front door then helped Matt to the sofa in the lounge. He flopped down in a heap, holding his stomach, still suffering from the occasional shooting pain.

"Can I get you anything?" She asked.

Matt shook his head.

"Would you like a massage? Abbey asked.

"That would be nice."

"I'll just get changed into something more comfortable." She hurried up the stairs, was there for a couple of minutes and returned wearing just a T-shirt and knickers. Matt's eyes nearly popped out of their sockets. She was carrying a bottle of something that looked like baby oil, which she put on the floor. "Right then, lie on the floor facing the ceiling."

Matt followed her orders. She then sat on top of him, being extremely careful not to put undue pressure on him. She picked up the baby lotion, and poured some on her right hand. She was ready! Matt felt extremely awkward. Her knickers were right in his line of vision and he did not know where to look. He decided that the best course of action would be to stare at the ceiling and think about anything but Abbey to save him further embarrassment.

She started to rub him, being extremely careful not to catch any of the staples. Her hands moved in a circular pattern, only just brushing his skin. Her touch was so gentle, her hands so soft, Matt was fighting like mad to think of something boring. Anything but Abbey. It was proving practically impossible. Abbey felt his erection against her bottom. She looked down on him, giggled and raised her eyebrows; he blushed and shrugged. He tried harder and started to relax, feeling drowsy. Her soft touch was sending him to sleep and the night's exertions had finally taken their toll. Within no time he had crashed.

Abbey stopped the massage and she gazed down at Matt. He looked so peaceful that she decided to leave him there. She went upstairs to the airing cupboard and pulled out a blanket to lay over him. When she came back down, she lifted his head and placed a couple of cushions under it. She then carefully covered him with the blanket, trying not to wake him, and kissed him on the forehead. Abbey decided to go to the kitchen. She was thirsty – a cup of tea would suffice. Once the tea was poured she sat in the kitchen and recalled the day's events. Both hands cupped the mug as she took small mouthfuls. It all started with Matt making the little girl feel special, that was amazing. His sad story about his cricket injury, maybe he could have had a career as a cricketer and onto a delicious meal and dancing before it ended in disaster with Matt ending up in hospital.

Once her tea was finished Abbey returned to the lounge area and turned on the television whilst holding the volume control on the remote to avoid waking her sleeping guest. She devoted the next few minutes channel hopping to find something she wanted to watch. She settled on a film, a romance. Throughout the film tears were shed as the will-they-won't-they scenario played out until boy wins girl's heart. Wiping tears from her eyes, she bemoaned the fact that real life was not as straightforward. Abbey yawned and noticed the time is was almost 4am. She glanced over to Matt, who was comatose. Rising from the armchair Abbey drowsily ambled over to the light switch, tapped on the dimmer switch and retired to bed.

Matt awoke and looked round the room for a clock. The DVD display read 8.30am: he had better get up. He felt extremely sore when he moved: his punishment for last night. The coffee table came in handy as a support as he pulled himself to his feet. He cautiously trekked to the kitchen, as he desperately desired a drink. He opened the fridge and scanned the contents – *Orange juice will do!* He removed the half full carton, located a glass and filled it.

Hunger struck next so an inspection of the cupboards was necessary. Some cereal was located in one above the toaster a bowl in a one underneath the toaster, a spoon in the drawer to the right of the sink and the milk obviously in the fridge. With everything located breakfast was prepared and consumed rapidly sitting at the breakfast bar.

After breakfast was consumed Matt returned to the lounge to watch some television. He tuned in to the sports news channel and there was a report on the cricket in Australia. Bruce Lawson had been at it again, with another double hundred to his name. Matt pondered what would have happened if he didn't suffer the elbow injury – would he be better than Bruce?

I'll check on Abbey, he thought to himself. The journey up the staircase was daunting, stretching tender muscles walking up and up to the top.

Abbey's door lay ahead. He knocked, but there was no answer. He entered, and Abbey was still asleep. He paused briefly to admire her beauty even first thing in the morning she looked resplendent. Matt tapped her on the shoulder, "It's 9.30am, what time do we need to be at the studio?"

She opened her eyes and yawned, "Morning. Not until 2pm, we've got plenty of time." She sat up, "How's the stomach this morning?"

"Fine. A little tender, but not too bad."

"Good." She patted the bed. "Now, come and lie with me; we can have another couple of hours' sleep."

She turned back the covers so he could join her. Matt hesitated: what exactly was her game? She slapped the bed again this time more forcefully. "What's wrong, Matt?" she asked. "Don't you want to lay with me?"

"Why are you doing this?" He looked puzzled. "You can't possibly have feelings for someone like me!"

She wanted to say it was because she loved him, that he had changed her outlook on life and made her realise that there was more to a relationship than status and good looks; love was all that mattered.

She paused: it was too soon. "No, don't be silly." She regretted lying. "I'm just being friendly because you helped me, and I think you're a nice person."

He was not convinced; there was some other motive, but what was it?

She gestured again, this time more impatiently, "Come on!"

He decided to join her anyway and keep his feelings hidden so they could not be used against him. She lifted up her left arm to enable Matt to rest his head on her shoulder. A subtle move by her meant his head positioned itself on her breast. She brought her arm down and gently pressed him tighter into her.

Abbey laid there deep in thought. How the hell would she ever be able to convince him? Was she destined to spend her life with someone who treated her like dirt, or could she make him see the truth? What could possibly change his views? Maybe it would help if she chatted to his best mate, he might have some ideas. That was a decision for later.

14

The telephone rang, waking Abbey. She decided to leave it and let the answerphone pick it up. She left it on constantly for the sole purpose of vetting the caller. If it was someone she wanted to speak to she could pick up and if she did not she could leave it running. It was Bully telling Matt to ring work as soon as possible and speak to Julia. Abbey put on her dressing gown and went downstairs to make breakfast. There was a lot of mail today, as well as the paper, and she bent down to pick it all up. There were mainly bills and special offers, which she threw onto the breakfast bar. She kept hold of the paper and read the headline, unable to believe it. 'MATT FINISH IN HOSPITAL'. The paper indicated that the reason for Matt returning to hospital was a brawl. Where did they get the information? Who was spreading lies?

She filled the kettle, made herself a pot of tea and sat down to read the paper. There were obviously no major news stories today as Matt had made the front page. Even the small run-in with the reporters was blown out of all proportion. The classic scenario was taking shape. They build you up, and then knock you down; the knives were sharpened and heading for Matt's back. She looked from the paper in dismay then saw his mobile. She walked over, looked towards the bedroom door to check if Matt was coming, and picked it up. She turned it on and accessed his phone directory. Would it be under Bully or his real name? Then she realised she did not know his real name, so her only hope was his nickname. She entered the first three letters and a number appeared. It was Bully's mobile – *thank God!* She rummaged around in her bag for a pen and paper and scribbled down the number. She switched off the phone and placed it back on the table; all she had to do now was find a convenient time to phone.

Matt rolled on to his stomach. *Ouch!* The pain was intense. He was now deeply regretting last night's boogie. He tried to lift himself up, but the pain was too much. The only way he was getting out of bed was to roll out. After a couple of unsuccessful attempts, he made it. Now all he had to do was negotiate the stairs.

Abbey heard him moving about and rushed up the stairs to help him. He eased himself on to one of the stools and Abbey passed him the paper.

"They've written a pack of lies about last night." She pointed to the front page. "There's not an ounce of truth in there!"

Matt's eyes nearly popped out of his head. "What a load of crap!" He turned the page with force, nearly ripping it.

Abbey knew how he was feeling. There had been

dozens of occasions when the Press had printed blatant lies about her.

"Can I get you any breakfast?" she asked, changing the subject.

The anger was slowly subsiding. "Can I have a couple of slices of toast please?"

Abbey removed two slices from the breadbin and placed them in the toaster, "Would you like marmalade or jam?"

"I'll have jam if it's seedless, raspberry jam if possible."

"As a matter of fact I have got seedless raspberry." Abbey walked over to the larder and removed a big jar of jam, "Are you always this fussy?"

"The seeds get stuck between your teeth." He pulled a funny face. "And they're buggers to get out."

The toast popped up, Abbey pulled them out and threw them onto a plate, as they were hot. She buttered the bread and passed him the plate and the jam.

"You can put the jam on." She put the knife in her mouth and sucked the butter off before handing it to Matt, "I'll probably put too much or too little on."

She cringed as he smothered the toast with thick layers of jam, "Would you like some toast with your jam?"

He was extremely hungry. All the food he consumed last night had stretched his stomach, which had the affect of making him even hungrier; it did not take long for him to finish his toast.

"Have you had enough?" she asked, "Oh, before I forget, Bully phoned. You need to phone Julia ASAP."

Matt looked worried. Had his Boss seen the article

and jumped to conclusions? It did not sound too good. She had not bothered to see how he was so far, so why now? It must be about the article.

"Can I use the phone please?"

Abbey nodded and passed him the handset. He dialled, slowly pressing the numbers as he tried to remember them. It rang; Bully answered.

"Matt, what's been going on?" he asked, "Julia's been on the phone to Head Office most of the morning, talking about you."

"Absolutely nothing." Matt felt the anger returning. "The papers made it up."

Bully put the phone on hold and rung Julia's office. There was no answer. He ran up the stairs to look for her: she was in the staffroom making tea.

"Julia, Matt's on line one."

She spun round to face Bully. "I'll take it in my office."

She left Bully to finish the drinks and went downstairs. When she entered her office, she opened a filing cabinet and pulled out a file, Matt's file. It contained notes made from her conversation with Head Office. She picked up the phone.

"Matt, what the hell have you been up to?" she asked.

"Nothing – the papers made everything up."

"Head Office doesn't agree. I want to see you to discuss this. You'll need to come back tomorrow!"

"It'll have to be tomorrow afternoon; I'm having my staples out in the morning."

"Fine, make sure that it's no later than 4.30pm."

She put the phone down. Matt had never before heard her be so abrupt. Head Office must have hauled her over the coals. What were they going to do with him?

"I'll speak to Dan, the show's producer," said Abbey, as she picked up the phone, "he'll sort it out."

Matt grabbed her hand to stop her from dialling, "Wait until we get to the studio!"

Matt went upstairs to get ready; having a quick shower and throwing on a t-shirt, trainers and tracksuit trousers (these were more comfortable than jeans and avoided the necessity of a belt, which would dig into his wound, causing a great deal more discomfort). Once he had dressed he went back downstairs and joined Abbey. She was waiting outside in the car, a black BMW convertible. It was spotlessly clean, both inside and out: she obviously took a pride in her vehicle. The engine was running. Abbey repeatedly revved the engine as if she was waiting for the start of a race. Matt jumped in, Abbey floored the accelerator and released the handbrake; the tyres smoked and the car sped off, screeching.

The journey took approximately twenty minutes. The studio was situated at an old abandoned airfield, and the perimeter was fenced off and patrolled by security guards. When Dan received the backing to make the series, he scoured the area for a suitable site to build a set. He wanted to make a show that would run for years and figured that by having its own set there would be fewer restrictions and greater flexibility when filming. He found the perfect site after a few weeks of looking, but could not afford the asking price. He thought about a backer, but was certain that nobody would be willing to shell out money on a new soap opera with no guarantee of success. Fortunately, Dan had been involved in many successful programmes previously and his reputation secured sufficient funds to buy the land and build the set.

The construction took two years from start to finish, forcing Dan to use his own funds to finish the project. There were times when he thought that the job would never be completed. The show had to start eighteen months before the finish of the set and at first; the show raised little interest from the public. Dan had constant battles with his backers to persuade them from withdrawing their support during the early stages. Viewing figures were not increasing and their patience was running out.

The show's fortunes changed dramatically with the introduction of two new male cast members: Craig Talbot and Paul Williams. They were complete unknowns but were a massive hit with female viewers. Figures sharply increased and the show became extremely popular. This had a positive effect: all the best writers wanted to work on the show, the storylines improved and increasingly people tuned in. Dan's project was saved. Everything slotted into place nicely; the backers were happy and continued to provide the necessary resources.

The security guard raised the barrier as Abbey's car approached and waved them through. They followed the road towards a car park. Abbey sounded her horn and a figure appeared from the front of the building. He looked like student, in need of a shave and a haircut or comb. His clothes had seen better days, but no iron, and his once white trainers were now grey. This was Dan.

He walked over to them and grabbed Matt's hand,

giving a firm handshake, "You must be Matt, pleased to meet you!"

"Likewise, Dan."

Abbey handed Dan the paper. "Have you seen this?"

Dan nodded, "Occupational hazard, I'm afraid."

"Well this crap could cause Matt problems. He's got to travel back tomorrow to face a hearing."

"Don't worry I'll make a few calls and sort it out." Dan patted him on the back in reassurance. "Abbey, you travel back with Matt tomorrow and I'll also phone your boss."

"I would really appreciate that, Dan."

"Go and get ready and I'll give Matt a tour." He waved her away. "Charlie wants to start shooting in an hour, so hurry up."

He put his arm around Matt and led him through the doors into the studio. There were many different rooms each containing different sets. The production crew were frantically working away, an adjustment here, an adjustment there, shifting camera positions and lighting until they were happy with the set up. The journey finished in the canteen: Matt had been shown around the entire building. He spotted the many familiar faces of the cast relaxing before they were needed. When Dan called out to them, they immediately stopped talking.

"I'd just like to introduce Matt to you all." He called one of the men over, it was Paul Williams. "Paul, I've got to go back on set; can you look after Matt for a while?"

"Sure."

Dan shook Matt's hand again, "I'll see you later to continue the tour." He rushed off, leaving Matt alone with Paul.

"Would you like a drink, mate?"

"Anything cold, orange juice if you've got it."

Paul nodded and called out to a lady behind the counter, "Sally… one orange juice, please."

She poured the drink and brought it over.

"Thank you," Matt said graciously.

"Come and sit down, I'll introduce you to some of the others."

Matt spent the next half an hour meeting the cast. They all seemed friendly and took an interest to him. He felt more comfortable around them than he thought he would. They were not as pompous as he had first imagined and certainly did not look down on him.

Suddenly the door flew open, and Craig entered with Abbey, "So this is the hero of the hour?" His eyes fixed on Matt, "I don't expect I need to introduce myself!" he claimed, confidently.

"Sorry, should I know you?" Matt laughed – was there anyone who did not? "Nice to meet you, Craig." He offered his hand to shake.

Craig did not appreciate anyone trying to make him look foolish. "I wish I could say the same." He ignored Matt's hand and sat down on a different table, visibly upset.

"Take no notice of him," Abbey said, "he doesn't like being upstaged."

She sat down next to Matt and asked him if he enjoyed the tour. He confirmed that it was very interesting and was looking forward to actually watching some scenes being filmed.

"I've got something better than that for you." She looked excited. "You're going to be an extra."

Matt nearly fell of the chair in shock. "Doing what, exactly?"

"It's only a small part; you won't have to do much acting." She reassured him. She could see that he looked uncomfortable with the idea. "All you have to do is say a couple of lines and sit in the bar… oh, and kiss me.

Matt stared at her, "What?"

"Come on lets get you to makeup," she pulled him to his feet, "and Dan will brief you there."

Matt resisted, but Abbey was not taking no for an answer. She pulled him towards the door as he gave up the fight. They arrived in makeup to find Dan waiting for them. He filled Matt in with the details: he would be dropping Abbey back after the funeral and she would kiss him goodbye. Someone else would drive the car and swap with Matt for the close up inside.

"All you have to say is, 'I got you back in one piece' and, 'See ya soon.'" Dan made it sound easy.

Matt wasn't as convinced. "What if I mess up, you could spend all day on this scene."

Abbey grabbed his hand, "You'll be fine! Act naturally." Matt practiced with her. She showed him how to say it and he copied. They did this about ten times until he did it right.

"That's great," she patted him on the back, "Just do it like that."

Matt was now ready for makeup. He sat in the chair

and watched in the mirror as the makeup was applied. He now looked younger and had a wig stuck on his head. It had been a while since he had seen that much hair.

"Right, let's get to work then." Dan was impatient.

He led Matt and Abbey to the outside set. Matt instantly recognised the row of shops and the pub used in every episode (these had also been built for ease of filming). In the distance, over on the left hand side, he could see the college grounds. It was not a complete building, just the front wall, and only one-storey high. This would explain why there were never many shots of the college, and certainly none from a distance. For the scenes inside, they either used sets in the main building, or used other locations. In fact, only the shops and the pub were complete constructions.

Dan led them to a car; presumably, this was supposed to be the car that belonged to Matt's character. It was an old, white, VW Golf – obviously his character wasn't rich. The camera crew were setting up outside the shops, where the car was to pull over. There were two cameramen posted on either side of the road, one in the middle of the road and one behind the car. This would enable Dan to select from a multitude of angles for the finished shot. The idea was to film from a distance until the car stopped and Matt would then replace the driver. The task of driving was down to an extra who was approximately the same height and build as Matt, and was fitted with an identical wig; from a distance, they looked identical.

Dan walked Matt back to his marker. He grabbed a megaphone and yelled to start rolling.

The car reversed around the corner, and then drove forward towards Matt. The cameras stopped rolling and he swapped places with the extra. They then moved closer to focus in on the two passengers. Matt felt extremely nervous and began to tremble, but Abbey had spotted his anxiety, "You'll be fine." She squeezed his hand in reassurance. "It'll be over before you know it."

Dan looked at the monitors conveying all the different angles and was happy with the set-up.

"Right, scene fifty-seven, take 1…" He looked around for signs that everyone was ready. "And action!"

Matt felt the tension build to an unbelievable level; his mind went blank.

"Cut!" Dan walked over to the car and stuck his head through the open window, "Relax, Matt, for God's sake!"

Abbey realised she would have to do something to relax him. Otherwise, the scene would take forever.

Dan called action, Abbey turned her head quickly and smashed it into the interior mirror, "Fucking hell!" she yelled. It worked! Matt burst in to a fit of laughter.

"Cut!" Dan's anger was building, "Jesus Christ! What next?" The crew began to laugh at Dan getting angry and Abbey rubbing her head. Dan's face softened and he started to laugh as well. After a few minutes, he called everyone to order and the camera's started rolling. The break certainly relaxed Matt. He was now able to deliver his lines perfectly – in one take – and Dan was satisfied.

"Thank you, Matt, that's all you need to do." He turned to the cameramen. "We'll continue with the pub scenes now."

All the equipment was shifted to the pub. The next

few scenes involved Craig and Paul having an argument and starting a fight, damaging the furniture and breaking glasses. Matt sat behind the camera and watched intently. These scenes were complex and took many takes before Dan was satisfied. Every time something went wrong, the broken furniture had to be removed and replaced, and glass swept away. Overall, a five-minute scene took two and a half hours to get right.

The rest of the day seemed to drag. After each scene, the equipment was moved from one site to another, inside then outside. Matt was getting bored with the constant changes, he could not put up with this every day; he would go insane.

At 6.30pm, Dan called an end to the day. Everyone appeared dead on their feet. Dan went up to Matt. "We're taking you both out for a meal tonight, as a thank-you. The limousine will pick you up at 8.30pm."

Matt nodded and went looking for Abbey; she had gone back to the dressing rooms to change. He knocked on the door. "Abbey, are you in there?"

"Yes, you can come in; I'm dressed."

He turned the knob and opened the door. Abbey was applying cleanser to her face to remove the makeup.

"We're being taken out for a meal tonight," he informed her.

"I know. Dan told me earlier." She threw the dirty cotton wool ball in the bin, "What time are they picking us up?"

"8.30pm."

"We'd better get back and change then." She picked up her bag and they headed for the car. When they got back to Abbey's house there was a message on her answer phone; it was Matt's mother, checking to see if he was all right. He returned her call and told her what he had been up to. Whilst he was on the phone, Abbey was upstairs picking out some smart clothes to wear. She decided on her long black dress, which she reserved for formal affairs, because they would be going to an upmarket restaurant, for sure. She called down to Matt, who had finished his phone call, "You haven't brought a tux with you, have you?"

"I don't even own one!" he replied.

She rushed downstairs, picked up the phone and dialled Paul Williams, the actor who looked after Matt earlier. "Paul, can you bring round your DJ for Matt, Dan's taking us out for a meal… great, thanks a lot." She put the phone down. "Paul will be around in fifteen minutes with his tux, answer the door 'cos I'll be in the bath."

Matt turned on the telly and, sure enough Paul turned up with his tux. "It should fit you, we're near enough the same height and build."

"Thanks a lot, Paul." He left after Matt had tried it on; it fitted perfectly. Matt settled back down in front of the telly until he heard Abbey unlock the bathroom door and enter her bedroom. He went upstairs and jumped in the shower.

They were both ready in plenty of time. Abbey looked stunning as usual and Matt was convinced nothing could disguise her beauty. He gave her his customary complement.

Matt felt uncomfortable in his clothes; it was not a

case of a bad fit, he just hated wearing tuxedos. Dressing up in this type of attire usually meant boring evening listening to the Bank's directors. He kept sticking his finger between his collar and neck in a nervous reaction.

Abbey brushed some dust from his shoulders and back. "You look very smart. It suits you."

The limousine pulled up outside Abbey's house and Dan stepped out. He asked the driver to sound the horn. It was Clive's night off so the agency supplied Bill Thompson, a retired gentleman who worked on occasions to supplement his pension. This was his first time driving Dan, but he appeared friendly enough and willing to involve him in conversation. There was nothing worse than driving people who felt too important to partake in a conversation with him.

The front door opened and Matt came out, followed by Abbey, who locked the door behind them. Dan met them halfway.

"You look very smart, Matt." He grabbed Matt's hand and shook it. "You're looking as gorgeous as ever, Abbey." He took her hand and kissed it. "Come along, the reservations are for nine." Matt got in the car and three people he had not seen before greeted him: one male and two females.

"Hello, I'm Matt," he gave them a broad smile. "You'll have to forgive me; I have no idea who you all are."

One of the women spoke, "I'm Judith Parry, the current writer. This is Charles, my husband, and this lovely lady is Margaret, Dan's wife."

Matt sat next to Judith and Charles, whilst Abbey sat next to Dan and Margaret.

"Where are we going tonight?" Matt asked.

"We're going to Cappelli's. It has the most amazing cuisine you'll ever experience, and we get treated like royalty."

Matt had heard of the restaurant. The Cappelli family had others throughout the country. They catered for the rich and famous, and charged extortionate prices in return for excellent service and high-quality food. Dan was right: they looked after their clients and spent the evening inflating their guests' egos. Although Matt had never been to one of these places before, he had seen them on various programmes.

They arrived at the restaurant and the concierge greeted them.

"Ah. Mr Majors, so nice to see you again, please come in." He walked over to the entrance and held the door open, smiling at all of them as they passed him. Inside the reception manager came running over to Dan.

"Mr Majors, we haven't seen you for a couple of weeks. We have your table waiting for you and your guests, right next to the piano."

"Thank you." He handed over a fifty-pound note. "You're rather quiet tonight."

"We had some important guests in earlier, Sean Bean and some Hollywood producers. They paid handsomely to restrict the number of bookings, but left about half an hour ago."

The privilege of being rich and famous, Matt thought, as the manager showed them to their table. The restaurant was fantastic. It had a marble floor and pillars, and in the centre of the room was a white grand piano with the tables spread out around it. Matt presumed that the nearer the piano the more expensive the table. The cutlery was gold and every table had candelabras in the centre. The dim lighting enhanced privacy. Abbey sat next to Matt, and Judith sat on his other side. He opened the menu and nearly choked when he saw the prices. Luckily, he was not paying, as it would probably cost a month's wages for an ice cream dessert!

The evening was very pleasant, especially as Matt became the centre of attention. People came over from other tables just to shake his hand and the duty manager supplied a complementary bottle of Don Perignon. Abbey was impressed with the way Matt handled it; he was very courteous and not at all big-headed. The more she learned about him, the greater her feelings grew. He was an exceptional person. He thought he was ordinary but he was the most extraordinary person she had ever met. Abbey could not think of a single fault, except his bloody-mindedness when it came to relationships.

Matt tapped his spoon against his wine glass and stood up. "I would like to thank everyone for such a lovely night tonight, but especially Abbey for looking after me. Cheers!" He raised his glass to salute everybody and took a mouthful of wine.

His speech received warm applause. Abbey stood up, waiting for her chance to speak as the applause finished.

"I would like to add my thanks to this remarkable person sitting next to me." She looked down at Matt. "He risked his own life to come to my assistance and thankfully stopped my attacker from assaulting me." She lifted her glass. "To Matt!"

Dan asked for the bill when they were ready to leave. Matt turned towards Abbey, pulling her to one side. "Do you know what I'd really like to do now?"

She stared into his eyes, was he going to kiss her? "What?" she asked.

"I'd like to go for a walk."

Abbey felt disappointed but tried not to show it.

"Why don't we then? It's a bit far to walk back to my house."

"I only meant a short walk through town then get a taxi," Matt explained.

"The doctor told you to take it easy. Aren't you still in pain?"

"I'll be fine! If I get the slightest twinge we'll stop immediately."

"OK, I'll tell the others."

Abbey informed them of Matt's plans and they said their farewells. Outside the night was very pleasant: cool, but not a cloud in the sky. Millions of stars twinkled as if they were winking at each other and the moon shone brightly to complement them. It was the perfect setting for a romantic walk. Matt looked at his watch: it was 11.30pm. He expected the streets to be busier, but only a few people were making their way home. Matt stared at Abbey. Suddenly he grabbed her hand, taking her by surprise. "Is it all right to hold hands? I'd like to pretend we're together."

Abbey wanted to say that there was no need to pretend and she would like nothing more than be his girlfriend, but she was frightened that he wouldn't believe her. "Yes, it's fine!"

They walked through the town hand in hand, with

Matt grinning like the Cheshire cat. Abbey squeezed his hand tightly then relaxed her grip and slid her fingers between his. She longed for him to take her in his arms and kiss her, but knew it was extremely unlikely, so she would have to settle for this first step. Her arms were getting cold, and goose bumps were starting to appear, so she used her free hand to rub her other arm. Matt noticed and immediately removed his jacket to wrap around her, leaving an arm around her.

"Right. Let's get you home, you're getting cold." He spotted a taxi and whistled to catch the driver's attention. Matt helped Abbey into the back and gave the driver directions. He put his arm around Abbey and she rested her head on his shoulder.

The taxi sped off, and they were home in no time at all, as there was hardly any traffic. Matt thanked the driver, handed him a tenner and told him to keep the change. Abbey pulled the house keys from her purse, put them in the lock and opened the door. "Would you like a coffee Matt? She asked, yawning.

"No thanks, I'm so tired. I think I'll go up to bed." He started up the stairs.

"Love you!" Abbey whispered, turning out the lights. She made her way upstairs, smiling. She had made progress tonight.

Matt got ready early in preparation for the district nurse. He had eaten breakfast, showered and changed into shorts and T-shirt before 7.30am. His thoughts turned to what would happen later at his hearing. He sat down and decided to watch television in an attempt to occupy his mind. He flicked through the channels impatiently; nothing seemed to interest him, until he reached the music channel. He lowered the sound to avoid waking Abbey. She had worked extremely hard yesterday and by the end of the meal last night, she was struggling to keep her eyes open. There was no reason to rush around anyway, as their train was not due to leave until 10.30am. Matt repeatedly checked the time, minutes seemed like hours. The early morning was really dragging and the television did not provide a sufficient distraction. Matt's thoughts kept returning to what lay ahead.

The doorbell rang, startling him. He looked at his watch: it was only 8.30am. If that was the nurse, she was early. Matt answered the door and, sure enough, it was the nurse.

"Mr Preston?"

Matt nodded.

"I'm Tracey Clark." She showed him her identity card. "I'm here to take out your staples!"

He stepped away from the door to allow her to enter. "Where do you want me?" he asked.

She pointed to the settee. "On there will be fine. Take your top off and we can get started."

Matt gently removed his T-shirt to reveal the staples. The nurse looked slightly shocked, "They didn't tell me I had to remove this many."

"It's not a problem, is it?" Matt sounded uneasy.

"No, I've just never removed so many in one go."

Matt laid down and closed his eyes. Tracey opened her bag and removed a funny-looking object, and a jar to in which to place the staples.

"Right, this may hurt a little." The nurse knelt down on the floor. "I'll take one from the top, then one from the bottom and so on."

She hooked the remover under the first staple and twisted it upwards: out it popped. Matt felt the tug, but it did not hurt – if they were all like this there would be no problem. He opened his eyes to watch. The nurse's hand shook, presumably because she had to remove so many staples. She attempted the bottom one using the same process, but it did not want to come out. She tugged harder; Matt winced. *That was definitely painful!*

"Sorry! I'm afraid there will be a few like that."

Matt's reaction increased the trembling of her hand, which made him feel more nervous. The whole process seemed to last an eternity. Some popped out easier than others; all with varying degrees of pain. Tracey breathed a sigh of relief.

"Do you want these?" She pointed to the staples. "Some people like to keep them as mementoes."

"No thanks, you can throw them."

The wound started to itch. Matt vigorously scratched it while Tracey put her tools back in her bag. She examined the scar and prodded around the wound for any sign of a reaction from Matt, but he remained unmoved.

"It's healed nicely." She wrote some notes on a pad. "Limit driving to small trips, once a day for a couple of weeks, and avoid heavy lifting. Your local hospital will call you in a couple of months for a check-up."

She placed the pen and pad back into the bag, picked it up and headed for the door.

"Thank you very much." Matt opened the door. She

smiled and walked to her car. Matt waved goodbye as she drove off, then closed the door. He rubbed his stomach; it was nice to be able to do that without catching any staples. His happiness was short lived – he remembered that he had to go back to London to face the music.

15

The noise of the door slamming woke Abbey. She rolled over onto her stomach to see the time: it was 8.50am. She had precisely forty minutes to get ready before the taxi arrived. She jumped out of bed and into the shower. She quickly washed her hair as well as her body and jumped out again – no time to relax.

The next stage was make up. She needed to create a good impression for Matt's sake. Whilst applying the finishing touches, she turned on the telly to watch the news. *Not much going on today.* Matt's hearing was more newsworthy than most of the stories. A cabinet minister resigning over cash for questions scandal; truckers' strike in France; these were the only real items of news.

All Abbey needed to do now was dry her hair and get dressed. She decided to place a band in her hair to keep it off from her face. The previous night she had pulled out a white blouse, black knee-length skirt and flat black shoes – she was going for the sensible look. She looked in the mirror: yes, she'd pass. The taxi sounded its horn; she had just made it in time.

Matt opened the door and picked up his bag, full of dirty washing. He had changed into his tracksuit trousers, as it wasn't the weather for shorts. Abbey came charging down the stairs, looking gorgeous and very smart; Matt would go home to get changed. He climbed into the taxi and Abbey followed. She smiled at him as the taxi drove off.

"Morning. What time did the nurse arrive?" she asked.

"8.30am."

"Let's have a look then."

Matt lifted up his jumper. *Without the staples, the wound looks great*, thought Abbey.

They arrived at the station with ten minutes to spare. Abbey went to pick up the tickets, whilst Matt picked up some magazines and newspapers for the journey. They met up at platform four, Abbey handed over the tickets for checking and they boarded the train. The journey home was uneventful. They both spent most of the time reading as opposed to talking and Abbey slept for the remaining journey, leaving Matt to contemplate his fate. Dan had promised to phone the paper for an apology and contact work to sort out the problem. The trouble was, would work still fire him?

As the train pulled into the station Abbey's mobile rang, waking her: it was Dan. He had phoned the paper and they would be printing an apology in tomorrow's edition. He had also left a message for Julia to ring him when the hearing had started. Hopefully, that would be enough to save Matt – he did not have long to find out.

When they arrived at the flat Matt had a quick shower and changed into his work suit, while Abbey polished his shoes. He looked extremely smart. As there was only a short distance between home and the office, they decided to walk. Everyone appeared to be shopping in London today and they had to fight their way through crowds of people, which added extra time to the journey. When they arrived, Abbey was asked to remain outside until they called for her. Julia asked Bully to take Abbey to the staff room and he duly obliged.

Abbey sat down as Bully put the kettle on. "Bully, can I ask you about Matt?"

"What would you like to know?" he asked, whilst searching for the teabags.

"How can I convince him that I have genuine feelings for him?"

Bully dropped the box of teabags on the floor. "What did you just say?" He could not believe it.

"I said—"

"I know what you said," he interrupted, "I just can't believe you said it."

"Why ever not?" Abbey asked.

"Because it's not every day that someone as beautiful as you claims to love my best friend, who, let's face it, is just an ordinary guy."

"I didn't say anything about love!"

"'Feelings' are the same as love in my book."

"OK, OK, but can you help me?" Bully was frustrating her.

"You picked the wrong person in Matt. Girls have really messed with his head in the past; he'll be a tough nut to crack."

Abbey was desperate, "There must be some way!"

"I honestly don't know." He handed her a cup of tea. "Have you told him how you feel?"

"No. Every time I try he comes out with something like 'famous and ordinary don't mix.'"

Bully wanted to tell her about Matt's feelings towards her but he decided against it. He thought it better that she find it out for herself, otherwise it would be obvious to Matt that he had told her; after all, only he knew.

"Just keep plugging away, wear him down, but remember, if you do anything to hurt him you will never – repeat, never – have another opportunity; he doesn't give second chances."

She thanked him just as Julia entered. "You can come in now, Miss Jones."

Abbey turned back and kissed Bully on the cheek; Bully blushed. *Why couldn't it be me?* he thought.

Julia led Abbey into the room where Matt was sitting opposite a man and a woman from personnel.

The man spoke: "Miss Jones, we have heard from Mr Preston and your producer, would you care to add your comments?"

Abbey told them exactly what had happened, that the papers had lied and that Matt was innocent. They listened intently to her, and when she had finished they left the room to discuss what action to take. Abbey looked at Matt; he looked extremely nervous. He was biting his fingernails, so she grabbed his hand and smiled to reassure him.

"It will be fine, I promise."

The panel returned and it was the woman's turn to speak. "Mr Preston, in light of the comments made today, from yourself and the others, we are prepared to overlook this incident." Matt looked at Abbey and smiled. "However, if the apology from the papers is not forthcoming, or you are involved in any further public acts which adversely affect the company's reputation, we will reconsider our decision."

"Thank you so much for believing me." Matt was ecstatic.

The man looked at him with contempt. "You ought to thank Julia, she has put her reputation on the line for you, young man."

Julia showed the Personnel Officers out, Matt and Abbey stayed seated. After a few minutes Julia returned, her face full of anger.

"Don't you dare do anything like that again!" she was furious, "It doesn't matter to them if you did it or not, you have damaged the company reputation."

"That's a bit harsh," Abbey said.

Julia did not bother to answer, she gave a stern gaze. *What would you know, Miss Celebrity?* She thought. "Now both of you get the hell out of here, I've got work to do."

Abbey and Matt got up and left the room as Julia slumped back into her chair – she did not want to have to go through that again in a hurry. As Abbey and Matt were leaving, someone called out: it was Bully.

"Are you in the clear then?" he asked.

"Certainly looks like it," Matt smiled, "but it was touch and go for a time."

"Are you going to be back for Graham's karaoke?"

"Yes, I'll give you a ring." He shook Bully's hand.

"Bye, Abbey." Bully winked at her to wish her luck. "Go for it." he whispered.

She nodded and gave him another peck on the cheek, then followed Matt out of the door. Bully looked on, full of envy.

"Right, we've got a couple of hours before the train back," Abbey rubbed her hands together, "What now?" Matt scoured the street for a taxi. As luck would have it, a vacant one was stuck in the traffic at the far end of the street.

"Come on, I'm taking you to my see my dad!" He started to run, as a puzzled Abbey followed; Norma said he was dead. They reached the cab and jumped in.

"Oak Hill Crematorium, please." They were going to visit his ashes!

En route, Matt asked the driver to stop at a florist's. He ran in and came out with a bunch of brightly coloured flowers. There were some orange; some yellow, some red and some white, to brighten up the surroundings. Matt climbed back into the taxi and they continued on their way.

Oak Hill Crematorium was on the outskirts of town and as a huge plot of land. The taxi dropped them at the gates. Matt paid the driver and arranged to be picked up in an hour. They walked up the road and past the car park, which was fairly empty as the majority of visitors came at the weekend. Abbey struggled to keep up with Matt's pace; he was in a hurry to get to his dad. They reached the crematorium and by the exit lay a vast array of flowers from a previous service. Abbey looked at them. One arrangement read 'Daughter,' with a message attached. It said: 'Left us for a better place, aged eight.' Abbey could not imagine losing a child so young. What must the parents be going through? She caught up with Matt, grabbed his arm and wrapped it around her. After reading the message, she was in need of comfort.

They wandered on through the gardens, with plots well kept and decorated with beautiful flowers that were smelling so fresh. Anyone at rest here was obviously well loved and frequently visited. Abbey was amazed a how beautiful such a sad place could be. She looked at Matt, but his face was revealing no emotion whatsoever. He obviously missed his father and Abbey wished she could have a close relationship with hers.

They approached a marble plaque, away from the others. The inscription read: 'To A Loving Husband and Father, Always In Our Hearts, Never Far From Our Thoughts.' There was a picture of a bat and ball carved into the marble, showing a passion for cricket. The plaque looked like new; it was obviously cleaned and polished regularly. There was an abundance of flowers, presumably from Norma's daily visits, Abbey thought. Matt removed his arm from around Abbey and sat down on the bench beside the plaque.

He stared up into the sky, his eyes full of tears. "Guess you know I nearly joined you, Pops," he spluttered. "Wish you were still here, we miss you so much."

He could not hold the tears back any longer and they trickled down his cheeks. Abbey stood in front of him, grabbed his head and pulled it in to her stomach.

"It's all right, let it all out." She could feel the tears moistening her shirt and sticking to her skin: she was close to tears herself. Seeing a man upset was a rare occurrence for her and not a pleasant sight. Matt composed himself and pulled away from Abbey's clutches.

"Do you mind if we just sit here for a while?" he looked up at Abbey, "And not talk."

Abbey sat down next to him and patted him on the knee, "That's fine."

He wiped his eyes and sat there in a trance, staring into space. Abbey stood up, knelt beside the plaque for a closer inspection, and read the cards. He must have had many friends, judging by the number of different messages. Abbey noticed a plastic bag in between the flowers, holding sheets of paper. She glanced back towards Matt, who was still deep in thought and decided to ask about them later. She rejoined him on the bench and put her arm around him. They sat there without uttering a single word for at least three-quarters of an hour. The only noise was an occasional sniff from Matt.

He eventually snapped out of his trance and turned to face Abbey.

"Thanks for sitting with me," he managed a smile. "When I'm here I just like to think."

"That's OK. What are they?"

Abbey pointed towards the paper in the plastic bag.

"Dad loved poetry, so I write for him."

"Can I have a look?" Abbey asked, intrigued, and picked them up.

He snatched them back off her. They were personal and he did not want her reading them.

"They're not very good," he said, reluctant to hand them over.

Abbey tried to grab them, but Matt hid them behind his back.

"Go on, I like poetry. Please?"

The way in she looked at him made it hard for Matt to refuse. He tutted and gave them to her. She carefully removed the pages from the bag, read the first sheet, then the second, and so on. Every so often, she glanced up at Matt and he could see she was moved. Her eyes were starting to glisten and a tear ran down her cheek. She sniffed and turned to the last sheet, as the tear dropped onto the paper; she carefully wiped it away.

Abbey struggled to speak, "They… they're… beautiful, Matt." She placed them back in the plastic bag and handed it to him, "Who is she?"

"No one in particular." He handed her his handkerchief to dry her eyes, "Someone in my head."

Abbey was not convinced, "Your descriptions are too detailed, it must be based on someone!" The anger was building inside him because he felt trapped into his answer.

"They are about you, damn it!" He shouted as the frustration pushed him over the limit, "Happy now?"

Abbey was so flabbergasted her jaw dropped; she was unprepared for that. Never in her wildest dreams did she think it could be her. She was so shocked she could not respond. She wanted to, she wanted to tell him how happy that made her feel because the feelings were mutual, and that they could have a future together, the words just wouldn't come out, no matter how hard she tried. She had missed this excellent opportunity.

Matt still felt angry at revealing his feelings. "Don't worry, I know that it would never work out and you would never feel the same way. Besides, it's only a stupid crush; I'll get over it."

He stormed off, leaving Abbey standing there in a state of shock. "Wait, I love you!" The words came out too quietly because the shock was still too much.

Matt noticed that Abbey had not followed him. He stopped. "Come on, we're going."

Abbey felt confused: on one hand she was ecstatic that he felt the same way about her, but on the other, she was mystified as to how she would persuade him that a relationship was worth the risk. She ran to catch him up. At least now, he had provided her with some hope, which gave her something on which to think.

They stopped off at Matt's flat to pick up some more clothes, before setting off for the station. Neither of them had said a word to each other. Matt still seemed embarrassed with his confession and Abbey was deep in thought about how to convince Matt.

On the train, Matt slept the entire journey as the events of the day had taken their toll. Abbey, on the other hand, was unable to stop thinking about what Matt had said at the crematorium; his words kept swimming around in her head. She was confused because his comments seemed to contradict his beliefs. Would he follow his head or his heart? She could not decide and it was driving her insane.

After almost two hours of continuous contemplation, she came to a decision: if he really wanted her, he would have to prove it. She had been in these situations before and had always been hurt. No matter how she felt, she would not push him; no matter how hard it was, it would ultimately be easier than rejection.

She woke Matt as the train pulled into the station. He yawned and stretched him arms far above his head.

He turned to face Abbey, "I'm sorry about earlier," he looked extremely embarrassed, "Forget what I said."

This was not what Abbey wanted to hear, but she had made her decision, "If that's what you would prefer."

Matt nodded and gave Abbey a broad smile, which she returned.

As soon as they returned to her house Abbey switched on the telly: there was a film on. She stretched out on the sofa to get comfortable. Matt went into the kitchen to make some coffee. He put Abbey's on the coffee table in front of the sofa and his on the floor by the armchair. The film was entertaining, a clever 'whodunnit': a powerful politician was believed to have committed suicide but was really murdered. The female detective was the only one to disbelieve the suicide story and fought alone to uncover the killer.

Abbey drifted of to sleep, she was so tired, but Matt did not notice. He sat there, engrossed in the film, and sipping his coffee. The killer turned out to be the Chief of Police. The female detective discovered that the politician had evidence to prove that the Chief of Police was selling drugs that had been seized and supposedly destroyed. He was about to blow the whistle on the operation when he was murdered. The end credits appeared on the screen.

"That was goo..." he turned round and noticed that Abbey had fallen asleep. She looked so peaceful; it would be a shame to wake her. Under normal circumstances, he would just carry her upstairs but as he was unable to lift anything heavy, he decided to fetch her quilt from her room. He walked on tiptoes up the stairs, pulled her quilt off the bed, brought it downstairs and covered her with it. He left her and went up to bed.

Abbey was dreaming about Matt. He had none of the hang-ups that she had come to know. He had taken her by surprise one day and kissed her without reason. Before she knew where she was, they were about to make love. He was slowly unzipping her dress whilst kissing her neck. The dress fell to the floor— *Bang!*

She woke up – it was the letterbox; the paper had just been delivered and she cursed its timing. It was just at the good part.

She threw back the quilt and walked over to the door to pick the paper up. On the front cover was the apology, only a few lines, but an apology all the same. Matt would be pleased, as his job was safe. Dan had obviously been persuasive. Abbey took the paper upstairs to show Matt. She burst through the door, smashing the wall with it, and achieving her aim of waking Matt; in fact, he almost hit the ceiling!

"What's wrong?" he asked, looking around anxiously.

“Nothing. You’ve got your apology.” She threw the paper on the bed. Matt grabbed the paper to see for himself.

“Excellent!” He was overjoyed. This confirmed his innocence; they would not sack him now.

The news gave Matt a boost. He appeared a great deal happier and more relaxed. He had an extra spring in his step, which pleased Abbey. For the last day and a half, he had been miserable because of the cloud hanging over his career. Seeing him back to his old self made a refreshing change.

They both decided to skip breakfast in order to get to the studio earlier so they could plan Matt’s last night in Manchester. Abbey only had a few scenes to shoot today but wanted to round up the usual gang before they made other plans. Matt had a quick bath, and changed into a tatty pair of black jogging bottoms and a long sleeve white t- shirt; Abbey had a shower and left her hair to dry naturally. They were both ready in record time.

Abbey tossed her car keys at Matt. “You can drive if you like.”

He caught the keys and smiled at her. “Excellent.”

Although outside it was overcast, and a strong wind was blowing, Matt put the top down. He jumped in and started revving the car as if he was on the start grid of a Grand Prix.

Abbey also jumped in instead of opening the door. “Just be careful.”

Matt raised his eyebrows and smiled. He pushed the accelerator to the floor and took off the handbrake, speeding down the road. He turned on the radio full blast and slowed to a sensible speed so that people could see him driving this flashy car. Abbey shook her head: typical man.

They arrived at the studio in one piece, surprisingly. The security guard lifted the barrier immediately so Matt did not have to stop. They made their way to the canteen, where the usual crowd had already gathered. Abbey clapped her hands, "It's Matt's last day on set today; he goes home tomorrow," she said, with a hint of sorrow in a voice, "Who wants to come out tonight?"

Most people had already made plans but the usual crowd – Craig, Paul, Ann and Siobhan – were up for a party.

"Right, what shall we do then?" she was keen for their ideas.

Craig had a thought, "Clubbing?" but his suggestion greeted with a total lack of enthusiasm.

"What about a pub crawl?" Paul asked.

Ann turned her nose up at the idea. "We'll spend half the night travelling!"

Abbey looked at Matt as if to say 'Here we go again'.

"What about the karaoke at the Good Intent?" Craig said excitedly, another chance to show off. Everyone seemed keen. Abbey looked over to Matt, "Is that OK?"

"Yeah, that's fine; I like a good karaoke."

Abbey breathed a sigh of relief: that was a lot easier than she had thought.

"Why don't we see if Dan will let us have the limo tonight?" Siobhan suggested.

"Excellent idea," said Ann, "I'll have a chat with him now."

"Be at my house for seven-thirty." Abbey instructed everyone.

Dan came in, with Ann in tow. He went over to the table and looked at Matt, "How would you like to do some more acting today? We've looked at your work from a couple of days ago and think we could add a few extra scenes for you."

Matt jumped at the chance, "Yes please! It'll look good on the CV."

"Great. I'll run through the scenes later." He grabbed a can of coke and returned to the set to organise the first scenes.

Matt and Abbey sat in the canteen waiting for nearly two hours. Abbey was strangely silent and Matt wondered whether his admission yesterday at the cemetery had made her realise she had been playing with his feelings with all her joke advances. The truth was, Abbey was completely confused as to how to play it with him. She knew he adored her but he still would not believe that ordinary people could have successful relationships with celebrities. She desperately needed some advice but so far had not had the opportunity.

"You're awfully quiet Abbey. Is anything wrong?" Matt asked. His voice broke Abbey's chain of thought. She had forgotten he was sitting with her.

"Sorry Matt." She thought of an excuse to mask her problems, "My contract is up for renewal in a couple of months, I was thinking whether or not to renew it." Would he buy it?

"Oh, right." *Funny, she'd never mentioned that before*, he thought, "Are you sure that's all?"

Just then, Dan returned to the canteen and joined them, before she had chance to respond.

"Right, Matt, what will happen is, your character will come looking for Abbey and tell her that you love her, and you want her come home with you. She will spurn you but she will be tempted. It will cash in on the romantic rumours that the Press started about you two."

"Hang on a minute," said a bemused Matt, "I'm not an actor. Whatever interest the Press has created will fizzle out once they see me acting. You'll probably have mass switch-off!"

"Abbey will help you through it. Just do what you did the other day." He handed Matt the lines, "Spend the next half an hour rehearsing."

Abbey looked at Dan in utter bewilderment. As he left she followed him out, "What the hell was all that about?" she asked.

"I watched that scene he did last night in the editing suite and came up with this idea. He's not a bad actor and there was a certain chemistry between you two that surfaced. It also gives me two options; if you decide to leave the series then he can be the reason, unless we kill you off, of course, or, if the viewers pick up on the chemistry, as I did, we can bring him back in."

Abbey was amazed: they would do anything for the ratings. Matt stood to potentially make an idiot of himself, to increase viewing figures, and Dan was not the type of person to change his mind, so she'd might as well get back to Matt and help him through it. Aware that time was not on their side, she rushed back into the canteen, where Matt was looking rather apprehensive.

“Don’t worry; just pretend it was yesterday at the crematorium.”

Matt looked at the lines. It was as if someone else had heard their conversation yesterday. He looked at Abbey, “This is practically the same as yesterday.” He thrust it in her direction.

“Then it should be even easier to act out.” She read the script. The only difference was the reaction of Abbey’s character.

They rehearsed repeatedly, but Matt could not inject the same feeling into his speech because the situation was staged and not for real. The more they tried it, the less confident Abbey became. She had to do something to make him angry.

“How was that this time?” he asked.

“OK, but you need to inject more feeling,” she knew she had to bide her time, “Come on let’s go to makeup.”

This time wardrobe provided Matt with a change of clothes as they felt that he would not wear scruffy jogging bottoms to meet a girl he was trying to impress. The same wig was fitted and Matt was ready. They walked onto the set; Dan checked that everything was ready and called for action. Matt did everything right until he said his lines: he was not believable enough.

Abbey decided it was time to act, “Stop rolling!” she yelled. “Listen, Matt, this might be a bit of fun to you but it’s my job and I don’t want to look bad because some nobody can’t act. You’re crap!”

“But…”

“I don’t want to hear any excuses, just put some effort into it!”

Matt's face filled with rage; he was seething. "I'm not a fucking actor!"

"Stop whining and get on with it!"

Everyone behind the camera was shocked at Abbey's outburst: it was unfair. Dan looked on in amazement, not quite knowing what to do. Matt glared at him, "Don't just stand there! Call action so I can get the fuck out of here!"

Abbey felt awful, but she was doing it to fire Matt up so that he would give a better performance, and, judging by his reaction, it had worked.

Dan called action. Matt was exceptional! He had made the scene completely believable with his rage. As Matt walked off the stage Dan called "Cut" and everybody applauded.

Matt looked round to see Abbey giggling and was not amused. Abbey explained herself: "I'm sorry, Matt." She gave him a hug, which he shrugged off. "I had to get you in a bad mood so you'd give a good performance. I didn't want you to look foolish."

He realised that he had been tricked and started to laugh, as did everyone else. Dan walked over to Matt. "Take my word for it, that was great. You looked like a professional." He patted Matt on the back.

"Don't ask me to do anything else – that was not a pleasant experience."

Dan agreed. "It's a shame, though, you could become a good actor."

"Enough," Matt placed his hands over his ears. "My acting days are over."

Matt went back to get changed and popped into the canteen to find Ann and Siobhan chatting.

"Are you looking forward to tonight, Matt?" Siobhan asked.

"Yes, it should be fun." He could smell lunch and looked at his watch, it was 12.30pm. He lifted the lid on the huge pan to confirm what his nose told him; he was right, it was spaghetti bolognaise. He grabbed a plate and immediately dished up a large portion for himself. As he returned to his seat, the others came in; lunch had been called.

Craig sat next to Matt. He leaned over to him and said, "Hang with me tonight and I guarantee you'll pull!" He winked and tucked into his lunch.

Abbey avoided Matt and called Ann over to sit with her, "Ann, I want your opinion," she spoke softly to avoid big ears, "I care for Matt very much and he adores me..."

"Do I detect a 'but'?"

Abbey stared down and the table. "But he feels that a relationship would be out of the question because ordinary people and celebrities don't mix."

"Has he specifically said that you and he could never work?"

"Not as such," Abbey tried to remember his actual words, "No definitely not."

"Well there's hope then?" which pleased Ann, "I trust that you haven't told him how you feel?"

Abbey shook her head, "No."

"If you really want him you'll just have to keep working on him."

Abbey thanked Ann for her help, but she was no clearer on how to proceed. What was she going to do?

Matt finished his lunch and returned to makeup to

change. He used a cleanser to wipe the makeup of his face. He found his clothes and changed back into them. As he left, he saw his reflection in the mirror: he had forgotten to remove the wig. A quick tug sorted that out. He was ready to relax for the rest of the day.

The afternoon session flew by. Everything fell into place, every scene was perfect on the first take; it was a director's dream. It was 4.30pm and all material had been shot. Dan thanked everyone for their hard work and switched off the lights: time to go home. Craig and Paul sped off in Craig's Porsche to get ready for the evening, whilst Ann and Siobhan freshened up and changed at the studio.

Abbey confirmed the arrangements. "So you'll pick Craig and Paul up first, then come and pick us up?"

She grabbed Matt's arm and pulled him towards the car park. "Come on, I've only got ten hours to make myself beautiful."

"Only three hours?" Siobhan asked sarcastically. "You may as well stay at home."

Abbey smirked and led Matt away. "7.30pm then?"

As soon as they returned to Abbey's house, she ran a bath and spent three quarters of an hour relaxing in it. Meanwhile Matt sat down with a bottled beer and turned on the TV. He selected the sports channel and watched an interview with Pat Keane. Keane had just signed an improved contract earning £250,000 a week. Matt was staggered: that was almost three times his annual earnings. How nice it must be to be paid to do something you love. If fate had not dealt him such a cruel blow, Matt would now be representing England at cricket. He would be their premier batsman, if not the world's finest. At fourteen, he had an average of seventy runs per innings in schoolboy's internationals. The next highest was fifty-nine, by the Australian Bruce Lawson. Their rivalry was intense; they were always trying to outdo each other, but off the pitch they were good friends. Matt remembered one match when Bruce scored 137 in the first innings. He then bet Matt that he could not beat that score. Matt reached 136, and gave Bruce an easy opportunity to catch him out, but he dropped the ball, which allowed Matt to score the two runs needed to beat Bruce's score. Bruce was furious. Those were the days, Matt thought. Bruce had gone on to play cricket at the highest level and was currently the world's best batsman.

Matt decided to go upstairs and sort out his clothes for the evening. He picked a cream jumper and black trousers, which, although not designer labels, were smart enough nonetheless. He called out to Abbey to check she was OK, as she had been very quiet in the bath. She had been deep in thought, still trying to decide on her strategy. She had decided to play it cool and see if Matt made any of the running.

It was 5.30pm, so Abbey climbed out of the bath, grabbed a towel and dried herself. She wrapped a smaller towel around her head, unlocked the bathroom door and made her way to the bedroom. Matt decided to run a shower, and as the water was exceptionally hot, steam filled the room and misted the window and mirror. He adjusted the temperature control to allow more cold through, then tested it again with his hand. That was better, now it was cool enough to enter.

Abbey sorted through her wardrobe. She wanted something sexy but could not decide what. Clothes were being discarded: too short, too long, too dressy, and too tarty. The wardrobe was emptying so fast that soon she would be swimming in clothes. Finally, she found a dress that was suitable: navy-blue, knee-length, low-cut and revealing, but not overly so. She pulled out a matching jacket, in case her shoulders and arms should get cold. *Perfect. My choice is excellent*, she thought. It was now time to put all the other clothes back in the wardrobe, as almost her entire wardrobe lay scattered on the floor.

Matt cleaned around the shower when he had finished, washing hairs down the plughole and rinsing soap off the sides. He went back to his room wrapped up in a bath towel and looked at his watch: it was 6.15pm. He could hear Abbey drying her hair so he decided to have a nap.

The limo pulled up outside the studio. Clive climbed out and went inside to find the girls. Siobhan was ready: she was wearing a black T-shirt and skirt and had placed her long, flowing hair neatly on top of her head. She never wore much makeup, so a little lipstick and eye shadow was sufficient. Ann was still applying her makeup. She was dressed in a red jumper and trousers, as skirts were not really her style. She preferred to keep her legs covered because of her slightly bulkier frame. Clive walked past and noticed Siobhan. He knocked on the door.

"Excuse me, madam, are you both ready?"

Ann picked up her lipstick and placed it in her purse – now they were ready.

"Come on then, let's go."

The limo pulled up outside Paul's house. Clive sounded the horn twice and after a couple of minutes, the guys came running out. Craig was wearing all designer labels: a black satin shirt and black jeans, and he looked the business. Paul, on the other hand, wore a white T-shirt and blue jeans – he was never one to get dressed up unnecessarily. The men joined the girls in the back and Clive started the journey to pick up the others.

Abbey knocked on Matt's bedroom door, "Matt…?" No answer. She entered the room to find him asleep. She gave him a little nudge, "Matt, wake up! The others will be here any minute."

Slowly he opened his eyes. He yawned and took a proper look at Abbey, "You look gorgeous!"

"Thank you." Matt's words touched her, "Now I think you'd better get ready."

She left the room to allow Matt some privacy and went downstairs to wait. A couple of minutes later Matt appeared at the top of the stairs. He came walking down, and at the bottom did a twirl. He looked very smart and smelled divine.

"I like your aftershave," Abbey remarked. "What is it?"

"Jean Paul Gautier."

Abbey heard a car outside and walked over to the front window to look out: it was the limo. The horn sounded, Abbey picked up her bag and ushered Matt out of the front door. Siobhan stuck her head out of the car sunroof and whistled. “Looking good Matt!”

Abbey threw her bag at Siobhan to shut her up and climbed into the car after Matt.

“Do you think that many people will be there tonight?” asked Craig.

Abbey glanced at the others as if to say ‘here we go again’. “Granddad said he was going to spread the word, so there may be a few.”

“Good. As soon as people know I’m coming the place will be packed.” Everyone groaned.

“You never change,” Paul replied.

Matt tried to imagine the feeling of being mobbed by crowds of people, but the idea did not exactly thrill him. He sat back hoping that it would not happen, but unfortunately he was just about to find out.

16

As the limo approached The Good Intent Matt noticed that there was a large congregation of people in front of the staircase that led to the room where the karaoke was being held. The bouncers, spotting the limo, cleared a pathway for the passengers to walk through. Craig opened the door and stepped out to the screams of the female contingent. No matter how many times he came here, the reaction was always the same; he loved it.

"Hi everyone," he shouted, and waved to the crowd, who responded with more screams.

Matt was next out, but the reception less hysterical; no screams, just applause. He nodded in appreciation and smiled. He was followed out by Abbey – a common occurrence of the past few weeks – who received a huge cheer and plenty of wolf whistles from the salivating males. The bouncers linked arms to stop the crowds from converging on the stars. Matt felt extremely uneasy. He had never been in between the crowds at events like this; he had always been part of them, desperate for a glimpse of the stars. He knew exactly how they were feeling right now.

Siobhan and Ann were next out, receiving rapturous cheers, and, lastly Paul, smiling as always, waving in all directions. They headed up the stairs to the karaoke.

Inside it was a very different story. There was no surge towards them; the odd few pens and paper waving, but the majority of people were used to them being there, so they were being treated as ordinary human beings, as opposed to stars. Matt started to relax. *This was better.*

They found a free table big enough to seat them all. Craig took the drinks orders and worked his way through the crowds to the bar, occasionally stopping to chat to friends. As the others sat down Abbey grabbed the book of available songs.

"What song are the Carlton College girls going to sing tonight?" Abbey shouted, flicking through the pages.

"That's if Craig lets anyone get a look in," replied Siobhan. She turned to Matt. "Are you going to sing tonight?"

"I've never sung at one yet, so don't hold you breath!"

Abbey looked at Matt; she knew him well enough to know that there was more chance of pigs flying, but hoped he would enjoy his last night with the cast. She was no nearer to breaking down his defences, in spite of his admission yesterday.

I'm going to enjoy myself tonight, she thought, resigning herself to the fact that the relationship was unlikely to happen, but she would worry about that later. She continued to study the book, looking for songs to sing.

Craig returned to the table carrying a tray full of drinks. "I've put a couple of songs in. Got to keep practising for my fans..."

The girls groaned.

"How many is that then, twenty?" asked Ann, smiling at the others.

"Very funny!" Her comments obviously annoyed Craig.

Abbey looked at Matt. "They've got a song here from the CD you lent me, one of my favourites: 'So Close', the unplugged version."

"That's unusual; you don't generally see many Hall and Oates songs."

Craig was listening to their conversation and had an idea: it might teach Matt a lesson and put Abbey off him, leaving an opportunity for Craig to make a move on Abbey. It was underhand, but Abbey was worth the risk. He left the table, pretending to go to the toilet and made sure he was out of sight. He opened the book on a nearby table, found the correct page and copied out the details, putting Matt's name at the top of the sheet. He picked up the paper, shoved it in his pocket and smiled: that would teach him.

The host switched on his mike. "Good evening everyone." He paused, allowing for their response. "Welcome to another Glen James night. Usual rules: I'll do a couple of numbers first to allow you all time to gain your confidence, or for Craig to find enough pieces of paper for his choices!" The crowd erupted in a fit of laughter; Craig gave him the finger.

Glen started to sing. He had an average voice, but

he stuck to songs that were not very taxing, which was sensible. He sang three songs and after his stint, he called the first person: Craig. He chose one of his favourites and was an excellent showman. He involved the crowd and his voice was ideal for the pop record. It would not be long before he dominated the charts. The trouble was, he knew it, but the women loved it… well most of them. Abbey and the girls appeared to be the exception. Craig finished his number to rapturous applause and screams from the crowd. He milked the moment, waving and thanking everyone. As he was leaving the stage, he took the piece of paper out of his pocket and handed it to the assistant. He whispered something to her, she nodded to confirm her understanding and he smiled as he joined the crowds. A selection of ladies mobbed him, but was happy: he had put his plan in motion.

Matt sat there reading the book. He flicked through page after page, looking at the different songs to see how many of his favourites were there. He wondered whether anyone would try to sing them. The girls were busy chatting away to each other, leaving him out of the conversation, but he did not want to discuss the sexy males that were here tonight anyway. Abbey was not the same with him since yesterday's revelation-was she backing off, fearing she was leading him on, or was she just embarrassed? Paul had already left to chat with some mates by the bar, obviously bored with the conversation too. Matt got up and wandered over to the bar to get another round of drinks. As he walked through the crowd people would shake his hand or pat him on the back: they had obviously been following the story in the

Press, although it would be hard to miss it, being front-page news in the tabloids for most the week. Still, it was nice to be appreciated.

"Abbey, don't you think we should talk about something different?" Ann asked, "Matt's just left us as well."

"Only to buy drinks." Abbey pointed to the bar, "Anyway, I want to see how he reacts if I ignore him."

"You don't give up, girl, do you?" Siobhan was amazed. "I'd have thrown the towel in long ago."

"You don't understand. Everything he does is so considerate, he's good with children, the only thing is he is so cynical about is relationships, especially those involving celebrities and non-celebrities."

"He's got a point though," Ann said, "It doesn't often work out."

"Don't let him hear you say that for Christ's sake," pleaded Abbey, "Now be quiet, he's coming back."

Glen called the girls to the stage, as it was now their turn. They had chosen 'Sisters Are Doin' It For Themselves.'

Highly original, Matt thought, *I've never heard women do that before!* They were very active on stage, a lot of bopping, but unfortunately, they sounded awful. Ann was singing way out of key, which affected the other two, but, still, they were enjoying themselves, unlike Matt, who felt like an outsider. He hardly knew anybody, and those that he did were ignoring him. He wished Bully was with him.

Paul noticed that Matt was sitting alone, so he went back to join him. "Sorry I deserted you," he said apologetically. "Craig bores me and the girls talk about blokes all night."

"Don't worry about me; I've got a drink, so I'll be fine. You go back to your mates."

"They're going to a casino soon and I can't go with them."

"Why not?"

"Because I have a gambling problem: if I go I could blow £10,000!"

Shit, Matt thought. That was a large chunk of his yearly salary, "How do you avoid it?"

"I go to Gamblers Anonymous three times a week."

The girls finished their tune and came back giggling. Someone else was making a fool of themselves now, and what a racket! The guy was so appalling that most of the audience were holding their hands over their ears. Listening to that was worse than having his operation without anaesthetic.

A few other people sang with varying degrees of success. The worst ones provided an injection of humour to the occasion. Glen sang another number, but this time he did not use the karaoke machine, he sang aided by a keyboard played by a colleague. He did two further songs, followed by Craig again, and again, and again-wasn't there anybody else who wanted to perform?

Paul spent most of the rest of the evening chatting to Matt, telling him of the various gambling exploits that at one stage threatened his acting career – he'd been given a final warning by the show's producers: stop gambling or find another job. It had worked, and they had even gone to the Gamblers Anonymous meetings with him. Their support gave him the determination to succeed and he had not placed a bet in over two years.

The end of the karaoke was fast approaching. Craig had just finished another song, probably his tenth, and took Glen to one side. "I gave you a request earlier for Matt, you know, the Londoner who helped out Abbey," Glen nodded, "Well he's ready to do his number now, can he go on next?"

He gave Craig the thumbs up. This was it: time to knock the baldy down. He smiled as he reached the table.

"You look like the cat that's got the cream," Siobhan remarked. "Why are you so pleased with yourself?"

"I've put Matt down for a song. He'll either bottle it or show himself up, and that'll show Abbey that he's not worth bothering with!"

"You bastard!" Ann was disgusted with him, "Siobhan, get Abbey!"

It was too late. Glen started his introduction. "Right, everyone, I want a big round of applause for the hero of the moment, who would like to sing for us now. Put your hands together for Matt Preston!"

Matt Preston! That's me! I didn't request to sing. Shit! What do I do? Siobhan reached Abbey and told her what Craig had done. She rushed over to Matt, "Matt it was Craig," Glen called out his name again, "You don't have to do it you know!"

"I'll give it a go." He got up and walked over to the stage. Abbey glared at Craig, who was pointing and laughing, and put her head in her hands. The crowd applauded as Matt arrived at the stage.

He whispered in Glen's ear, "I've been stitched up, what am I singing?"

"'So Close', the unplugged version. Ready?"

Matt nodded and cleared his throat. The music started, he took a deep breath. The intro finished, then the first words appeared on the screen.

Abbey could not believe her ears; they must be playing a trick on her. Matt must be miming – it was Daryl Hall singing. She looked around her and everyone looked shocked at how good it sounded. Just then, Matt made a slight mistake; he got a line wrong, so it really was him singing. He was fantastic, brilliant! His voice made the hairs on the back of Abbey's neck stand up and she could feel the whole of her body covered in goose bumps. Her mouth dropped open: how the hell had he kept this gift from the gods a secret?

She wanted to cry, nothing had ever moved her like this before. She could love him for his singing alone. Matt had really cast a spell on her; she was hooked. All Abbey could do was stand and marvel at the sound of Matt's voice.

Ann walked over to Abbey. "Did you know he could sing like that?"

She got no reply. Abbey just stood staring at Matt, starry-eyed. No one spoke a word in the whole room; everyone was focusing on Matt, amazed at the sound of his voice. He was giving it everything. The veins in his throat looked ready to explode, yet he was singing with a smile on his face, obviously enjoying every moment. Abbey started to move forward, she wanted to be in the front row. Matt's voice was like a homing beacon, drawing her in. When the song finished, Matt received the loudest applause given all night. He glanced over to Craig and smiled, but Craig looked furious, as his plan had seriously backfired.

Glen walked over to take the mike from Matt. "Wasn't that brilliant everyone, eh?" He called for even more applause. "Where the hell did you learn to sing like that?"

"I used to be in the school choir," Matt gasped, waiting for air to return to his lungs. "I fancied the music teacher so I stayed behind for extra lessons."

The crowd roared with laughter: a schoolboy crush had helped develop this fantastic voice.

"Do you sing in a band?"

"No, my mate and I have sung at a few weddings but that's all."

"I tell you what, how about another? Would you all like to hear Matt again?"

Another round of applause broke out – a positive sign.

"OK then, can I use your keyboard?"

Keyboard? He can play the piano too? Abbey was eager to here this one.

She climbed onto the stage and stood next to the keyboard. Matt winked at her, "This one's called 'I Ain't Gonna Take It This Time.'"

This was her favourite song from the album. Matt made room on the stool for Abbey to sit, so she sat down, unable to take her eyes off him. She was even more smitten than before. Matt played the introduction, hammering his fingers against the keys for a pronounced effect.

What an unbelievable night. Matt was brilliant again. The song required a tremendous amount of vocal energy, which Matt provided in excess. The crowd started to clap in time with the music. Craig had seen enough and stormed out, nearly bumping into Pat Keane, who was just arriving.

Pat saw Abbey on stage. *So, she had muscled in on her saviour? She didn't waste much time.*

Matt finished and got another huge round of applause from the crowd. Abbey wrapped her arms around him and planted a kiss on his cheek. "Why did you not mention this before?" she seemed almost angry. "You certainly are a man of many surprises. You were magnificent!"

"Here, here!" Glen added, "Who are you signed to?"

"No one, I'm not good enough to make it my living!"

"I think you could." Glen was confident, "You could always work with me. We'd make a fortune; everyone would come to listen to you!" He handed Matt his business card.

"Thanks, but I don't think I'm cut out for it."

Matt shook Glen's hand and walked off with Abbey, then bumped straight into an angry-looking Pat.

"I wouldn't bother, mate, she's boring, and when she eventually shags you, it's nothing special."

"What's your problem?" Matt asked. "You dumped her; she didn't dump you."

Pat thrust his face in front of Abbey's. "You're a prick teaser. You wanted me as a meal ticket."

"That's not true," Abbey's eyes were filling up and a tear trickled down her cheek, "I loved you, but you treated me like dirt!"

"Bullshit!" he screamed. "You were only interested in my money."

Abbey ran off, sobbing. "Wait!" Matt tried to grab her but missed. He turned to face Pat, "You may be a great footballer but you act like a fucking wanker !"

Pat saw red. His face full of anger, he threw a punch at Matt, who side-stepped it and landed a left hook to Pat's jaw. He hit the floor in a flash. Matt stood over him.

"Don't ever try that again," he growled. "If I ever see you bothering Abbey you'll feel another fistful, understand?"

Pat nodded, though his pride was dented. Matt walked out calmly, while a bystander helped Pat to his feet. "You deserved that, mate," he said.

Matt went through the door to see Abbey standing facing a wall, sobbing. He walked up behind her, and she turned round and threw herself into his arms. He held her tightly, stroking her back, trying to console her.

"Don't cry; that bloke's an arsehole!"

Abbey gripped him tighter. "What he said is not true."

"Come on, let's get you home," Matt turned to face the road, keeping one arm around Abbey. "Taxi!"

A taxi stopped. Matt opened the door for Abbey and told the driver the address, before climbing in beside her. No one spoke on the way home, Abbey just nestled her head into Matt's neck, still crying. He felt the moisture of the tears against his neck. The more he felt, the tighter he held her. The taxi arrived outside Abbey's house. She got out and dug around in her bag for her keys. She pulled them out, sniffed back some tears and opened the door. Matt paid the driver and followed her in.

Abbey stood waiting just inside the door as Matt entered, "Hold me, please," she pleaded, and Matt had no choice.

She stared him straight in the eye, tears still in full flow, "You really are someone special, Matt."

He raised his hand to her face, gently wiping away the tears from her cheek. He smiled. "You're not too bad yourself."

Abbey managed a smile, her eyes focused on Matt's. She tilted her head slightly, slowly edging her face closer to Matt's. She paused for a second, with her mouth open. She edged closer until her lips touched Matt's and they kissed, Abbey's mouth opening and closing around his. Matt gave as good as he got. Abbey tightened her grip on Matt. He placed his hand on her face, still kissing her, and Abbey's heart was melting. The intensity of the kiss was reaching fever pitch.

Suddenly Matt broke away, pulling himself free of Abbey's clutches. "This isn't right; it's happening for the wrong reasons."

"You're wrong. Seize the moment, take me." Abbey was practically pleading with him, "Please, I have needs too."

Matt had dreamed of this moment from the day that he had first set eyes on her. He looked into her eyes – they were full of hope, pleading with him. He reached out his hand towards her head. He ran his fingers through her hair and kissed her again. The longer their lips touched the more intensive the kiss became.

Abbey hung her arms around Matt's neck as if her life depended on it. His hands moved up and down her back;

hers moved down to his waist. She lifted his T-shirt and pulled it off, exposing his chest; she threw it to the floor.

Matt's hand moved down Abbey's back until it reached her zip. He pulled it gently, slowly undoing it whilst the other hand took care of the button. Abbey's dress fell to the floor, exposing her underwear. Abbey pulled away from Matt. She grabbed his hand and led him upstairs to the bedroom, shutting the door behind them. The rest of their clothes came off, skin touching skin. They made love softly, gently, and passionately. This was the greatest experience of Matt's life. If he died tonight, he would die a happy man.

Maybe a relationship could work between us, he thought. He looked over to Abbey; she was fast asleep, but she was smiling. He had misjudged her. For some unexplained reason she wanted him. This time he was sure, there was no way she would treat him like his previous girlfriends. He smiled, put his arm around Abbey and drifted off to sleep.

17

The radio switched on: it was 7.30am, time to get up. Abbey opened her eyes and looked at Matt. He lay still, fast asleep, with his face pressed against the pillow. Abbey sat up, and looked again; he seemed so peaceful. Last night had been fantastic. Matt must now realise that she was in love with him; surely, the struggle was over.

Abbey climbed out of bed to get the newspaper that had just dropped through the letterbox. She tiptoed down the stairs to avoid waking Matt. She reached down to pick the paper up, and as she unfolded it and looked at the headline, she nearly dropped it in disbelief. Splashed across the front page was an article about a brawl between Matt and Pat in the pub last night, suggesting it was over her. She glanced up towards the bedroom, was it true? If it was, Matt would be in serious trouble at work; they were still contemplating his position after the last episode.

Abbey showered and changed into jeans and T-shirt; ready to go to the studio. Matt was still asleep so she decided to leave him a note and the car keys so he could make his own way to the studio later. She left the note on top of the newspaper, picked up the phone and arranged for a taxi to pick her up.

A horn sounded outside. Abbey looked out of the window – it was her taxi. She wished that she did not have to work today. All she wanted to do was spend the day in bed with Matt. She was totally smitten and positive he felt the same. She picked up her bag and rushed out to the taxi.

The noise of the door shutting woke Matt. He moved his arm over to Abbey's side of the bed to give her a cuddle. He felt around, but she was gone! Why did she not wake him? He climbed out of bed and went to the toilet.

"Abbey!" he called down the stairs: no answer. She must have already left for work.

He had a quick shower and dressed in his jeans and a thick jumper, as it looked rather cold outside. He went downstairs and spotted the note on top of the paper. He picked it up and read it:

'Didn't want to wake you. See you at studio later. Left the car for you. See you later, love Abbey.'

That was a particularly cool letter after last night's events, Matt thought. Abbey seemed to enjoy it, so was she now regretting it? He glanced down at the paper and saw the headline, 'PRESTON NOT SO KEANE ON PAT!' He put his head in his hands. *Jesus! I'm finished. They will definitely fire me now.* He slumped back into a chair, what was he going to do now?

As Abbey arrived at the studio, Siobhan greeted her, "You missed all the fun last night," she said excitedly. "It's front page news!"

"It couldn't have been that bad. Matt came out to find me only minutes after I'd left."

"It wasn't. Pat threw a punch, which Matt avoided, then Matt knocked Pat over with the only other punch."

"It will probably result in Matt being fired all the same," Abbey said, sadly, "I wish I could do something to help."

"Maybe you can," Siobhan said triumphantly, "You heard him sing last night, he was brilliant."

"So?" Abbey looked puzzled, "What are you getting at?"

"Fix him an audition with a record producer."

"I don't know any!"

"No," Siobhan smiled, "but Craig does."

Abbey looked at her and winked. "You're brilliant! Oh, I've got some excellent news."

"What," Siobhan was intrigued, "Hurry up, tell me."

"We made love last night."

"Really?" Siobhan wanted more. "What was it like?"

"Fantastic! He was so gentle and considerate." Abbey recalled every detail in her mind, "I'm sure now that he believes the way I feel about him and he's not just being used."

"I'm so pleased for you both."

Matt had to know what was going on. He phoned work and, luckily, Bully answered, "What's happening there?" Matt asked.

"I think you're up a creek without a paddle." Bully sounded concerned, "Julia's in a foul mood. She totally ignored me and she had a call from Head Office, which lasted over half an hour. She came out even worse. Looks like bad news, mate."

Matt put the phone down. Nothing could be done. At least he had Abbey; she would help him find another job. Maybe he could work as an extra?

He opened the front door and peered out. No reporters, thank God. The car was out on the driveway, so he unlocked it and sped off towards the studio.

The journey only lasted about twenty minutes as there was no traffic on the road, and Abbey's BMW could really shift. Security greeted him at the gate, "Morning, Mr Preston. Last day with us today?"

"Should be; I've got to be in London tomorrow."

The security guard raised the barrier and Matt drove in and parked. He could not wait to see Abbey and tell her how wonderful last night was, and that he would like to see her on a permanent basis. He headed for the dressing room area.

Abbey knocked on Craig's door. "Enter," he said, arrogantly.

"Well, well, well," he said smugly, "What can I do for you?"

"I need your help." She hoped not to have to resort to begging. "You heard Matt last night… he's talented!"

"Not bad."

"Will you speak to your producer and get Matt an audition, please?"

Craig shook his head, "Why should I help him? What's he going to do for me in return? Nothing, that's what."

"Can't you just do it out of kindness of your heart?

If the shoe was on the other foot, he would do it for you without hesitation!"

Craig remained unmoved.

"We've all needed help at some stage, even you. Or have you forgotten how you started."

Craig thought back to his big break. She was right! But why should he help this nobody. Matt didn't appear to want the lifestyle.

"Please," she started to beg, "I'll do anything!"

"Sleep with me then!" he demanded.

Matt heard voices' coming from Craig's dressing room: Craig's and Abbey's. What was she doing in there? The door was open, but he waited outside, only to here Abbey's response.

"OK, I'll sleep with you."

He could not believe his ears! She was all over him last night, now she was moving on to Craig. His heart sank. Another bloody bird using him. For what purpose? He turned round and headed for the canteen.

The conversation was far from over.

Abbey had not finished her sentence, "After you make the call to your producer."

"OK, OK I'll do it now." He picked up his mobile and dialled the number. "Hi Wendy, can I speak to Paul, please?" There was a long silence. "Paul, I've seen a singer who I think you'll be interested in. When can you see him?" Another long pause. "He lives in London anyway, so I can't see it being a problem. I'll bring him along then. OK, bye." He switched off his phone,

"Tomorrow 3.30pm. Right. Come on then, let's get to it."

"Not now," Abbey said, stalling, "After we've finished today. You want more than five minutes worth don't you?"

He nodded. "You're right, we've got to be in makeup in twenty minutes. After work it is then."

Abbey was delighted. She had got Matt an audition that he would sail through, and he could then forget his hang-ups about them being from different worlds as there was no doubting he would succeed. Abbey was so excited; she wanted to tell Matt immediately. This was her chance to show him just how committed she was to him. Where was he?

Matt felt used. This was exactly what had happened in every relationship he had ever had. Why did this keep happening to him? In the canteen, Siobhan and Paul were drinking when Matt entered. He walked over to join them.

"Hi Matt. Looking forward to going home?" asked Siobhan.

Matt ignored her. All he could think about was what Abbey said to Craig: '*I'll sleep with you, I'll sleep with you, I'll…*'

"Matt!"

"Er… sorry, I was miles away." He did his best to hide his disappointment.

"Are you looking forward to going home?"

"No, not really."

Abbey entered, with Craig following behind her, "Oh I'm glad you're here, I've got some wonderful news."

"What's that then?" Matt really could not care what it was.

"You've got an audition tomorrow with Paul Sullivan, Craig's producer. In London," Abbey was ecstatic. "It's at 3.30pm. Is that OK?"

"Yes it's fine." He was not really paying attention. This was Abbey's way of dumping him without any guilt.

"You're gonna walk it." She gave him a hug, which wasn't reciprocated, "What's wrong, Matt?"

He was not about to reveal his feelings, "I'm worried about work, that's all."

Abbey thought it strange that he had this excellent opportunity, yet was worried about his job. He would nail the audition so the job wouldn't matter. Was there something else troubling him? He appeared to have reverted to his old self.

"I'll pick you up at 3pm then," Abbey said.

"No, I'll meet you there."

"You know where to go?" she asked

"Yes. Right, I must be getting back – my train's in forty-five minutes."

Matt said his goodbyes, giving Abbey a hug and a kiss, and left the building. Clive was waiting outside, ready to drop him at the station. Matt loaded his belongings into the boot and climbed in the rear. He was desperate to get away from this nightmare.

Back in the canteen, Abbey seemed concerned, "Did he seem all right to you Siobhan? I thought he'd be more excited."

"He was acting strangely," Siobhan shared Abbey's

view, "I asked him if he was looking forward to going home and he ignored me. I had to practically yell to get his attention."

"Probably pissed off having to go back without me," Abbey was desperately trying to reassure herself, "Still, we'll see each other tomorrow."

Abbey called Craig over. "Everybody, I've got an announcement to make:" she put her arm around him, "Matt has got an audition tomorrow, thanks to Craig."

Everyone began to applaud, "Before you continue, there is a condition attached: I have to sleep with him!"

There were rumblings from the gathered crowd and Craig wanted the ground to open up and swallow him.

Abbey turned to face him, "I'm sorry to disappoint you, but I won't sleep with you. Consider yourself tricked."

Everyone laughed. Not only had Craig been rejected, but he had also been made to look foolish. He stormed out to cheers from everyone. He had learned a valuable lesson: do not mess with Abbey.

"One last announcement everyone," Abbey decided to let her feelings out, "I'm in love with Matt and I think he feels the same, and that's one of the reasons for the audition."

Ann rushed over to give Abbey a hug. "He seems perfect for you. I'm delighted for the both of you."

She slowly received congratulations from everyone in the room. Now her feelings were out in the open, she prayed that Matt would not reconsider.

Matt spent the entire journey to London deep in thought. He could not believe the events of the last twenty-four hours: they were making love one minute, the next she was jumping into bed with someone else. Why did he always fall for the same old tricks, time after time? He decided to boycott the audition tomorrow. Why should he go to ease her conscience? Maybe he would be a success, maybe he would not. He was not prepared to find out.

The train pulled into the station. Matt collected his belongings and joined the queue to disembark the train. His mobile rang: it was Bully.

"Where are you?"

"Just getting off the train now. Meet you in the pub in half an hour."

"I'm already there, mate."

Matt entered the bar to find Bully chatting to Terry. "Pint please, Terry."

"You look pissed off, man!"

Bully passed Matt his drink, "What's up?"

Matt downed the pint in one go, "Long Story. Another time, maybe." He shook the glass, gesturing to Terry to give him another: he obliged. Matt knocked it straight back again.

"Steady on, Matt, it's only 6.30pm." Bully attempted to snatch the glass off him.

"This morning I was on top of the world. Then, I find out the bitch is planning to sleep with someone else." Matt slammed his empty glass down on the bar.

"Sleeping with someone else?" Bully was confused. "Are you trying to tell me you shagged her?"

"Yep," he waved his glass again, "Not that it meant anything to her."

Bully smiled, “Who gives a shit, you shagged Abbey Jones, ‘Sex Goddess’!” He was so envious.

“I suppose so,” Matt’s ego was slightly boosted. “I just can’t believe it’s happened again: a women shits on me.” He started his third pint.

“You could sell your story to the Press, make a fortune!”

The discussion on the best course of action to take carried on for most of the evening. Finally, they moved on to the subject of work.

“Julia wants you to come in tomorrow morning.” Bully looked uncomfortable, “I think she’s being forced to sack you.”

Matt gulped, his problems compounding by the minute, “If that’s the case then I’m glad. I hate the fucking job anyway!”

“What will you do?” Bully asked.

“I was offered a job by this karaoke singer in Manchester,” Matt pulled out a business card, “I might give him a call.”

Bully nearly spat out his mouthful of beer. “You sang at a karaoke night?” He was completely stunned.

“Yep.”

“What did you sing?”

“‘So Close’ and ‘I Ain’t Gonna Take It This Time.’”

“I wish I was there to see it!”

Matt finished off his sixth pint, and by now he was completely drunk. “Great buzz,” his words were slightly slurred, “never felt anything like it. Total strangers cheering and applauding me.”

Bully patted him on the back, “Come on, sunshine, it’s time to get you home.”

Matt started to walk, but his vision was impaired, making him sway from side to side. The inevitable happened and he fell over.

"He'll never make it home in this state," Terry said, helping Matt to his feet, "He can stay here tonight. Help me get him upstairs."

They struggled to get Matt into a spare room. He was a deadweight and no help to them, only managing laughter. They threw him on the bed and shut the door behind them. As soon as Matt's head touched the pillow, he was fast asleep.

"I'd better get going, Terry – work tomorrow."

"All right, mate," he shook Bully's hand, "Coming to the karaoke tomorrow?"

"You bet. I'll probably sing too!"

Terry couldn't believe his ears. "That'll be a turn up for the books."

"Well now Matt's done it I can't let him be one up on me, can I?" He descended the stairs and left through the rear door. Terry returned to the bar to ring the bell for last orders.

Abbey put down the phone. She had arranged to meet Craig tomorrow at the station at 9am to catch the 9.30am train. She could not wait to see Matt again. She would reveal her feelings to him and was so excited. The phone rang: it was Sonya.

"Got your message. What's up, Abs?"

"I'm so happy," she was positively glowing, "Matt and I made love last night."

Sonya nearly choked on her coffee, "What, you managed to break his resistance? Fantastic."

“It was the best sex I have ever had,” she revealed, “He was so considerate and so gentle, he sent me wild with desire. God I love him!”

“See what you’ve been missing?” Sonya said, “These famous people are only interested in satisfying themselves.”

“I’m coming to London tomorrow. Matt’s got an audition.”

“For what?”

In all the excitement Abbey forgot to tell Sonya about the Karaoke, “Matt sang last night and he’s got one hell of a voice,” she said, almost bursting with pride, “I managed to trick Craig into arranging an audition.”

“Trick him?” Sonya asked.

“He said he would only arrange it if I slept with him,” Abbey giggled. “I made him phone first then I told everyone what he said. He was so embarrassed.”

“Shall we meet up in the evening then, Abs?”

“Yes. We’ll go to Matt’s local, ‘coz I’m sure he said there was a karaoke on, so you can hear him sing.”

“Great. Be at my place at 7pm tomorrow. Bye.”

Abbey replaced the handset. She could not get Matt out of her head; tomorrow could not come around fast enough.

18

The smell of bacon wafted into the bedroom, reaching Matt's nose. As soon as the scent registered, Matt woke up. Where was he? It suddenly dawned on him: last night, too much drink. Terry obviously took him upstairs as he had on several occasions in the past. He felt very fragile, not hung over, but very close. He clambered out of bed and followed the smell to the kitchen.

"Morning," Terry stood over the cooker, "Made you a good old fry up. Sit down mate."

How the hell could he be so cheerful this early in the morning? Terry dished up two slices of bacon, two sausages, baked beans and a fried egg and put it on the table in front of Matt.

"Thanks." Matt picked up his knife and fork and started to cut up the bacon, "Thanks for letting me stay." He took a mouthful of food.

"I couldn't let you leave in that state, could I?"

Matt swallowed his mouthful. "I guess not."

"I caught some of your conversation last night," Terry sounded concerned, "want to talk about it?"

"Well, I love someone who I thought felt the same way and I'm probably going to lose my job. What's there to talk about?"

"How do you know she doesn't feel the same way? Have you asked her?"

"No, I heard her agree to sleep with someone else."

"Oh. Are you sure you couldn't have made a mistake?" Terry was hoping.

"How can you mistake 'OK I'll sleep with you'?"

He had a point. All the evidence was there, but it just did not ring true from the other information he had heard about Abbey. Terry had known him to make mistakes about people.

"Are you going to see your boss today?" Terry asked.

Matt finished his last mouthful, wiped his face with a serviette. "I think I'd better."

Terry stood up, took Matt's plate and placed it in the sink. He turned round, "You can work for me until you get back on your feet."

Terry felt a great deal of responsibility towards Matt and would always be on hand to offer advice when required. He had never had a son and Matt was the closest he would ever get. He also promised Matt's father, a good friend of his, that after his death he would look out for Matt.

"That means a lot to me, Terry, thanks." Matt was touched.

Matt went home to change and make himself presentable. He dressed in his best black suit and walked slowly to work. He felt as if he was walking to his own execution. It was extremely nerve wracking. In half an hour, he could be out of a job, because of Abbey. He wished that he had ignored her scream – life would have been a lot simpler.

On arrival, Matt had to wait in the banking hall until Julia, the manager, called him. She was on the phone so Matt had another agonising wait to find out his fate. Bully was nowhere to be seen, although he said that he would be in today. He must be upstairs.

Julia came down, her face like thunder.

"Come through to the office Matt and have a seat." Her tone was very assertive.

Matt sat down, preparing for a complete dressing down.

"I've just come off the phone to Head Office," her face filled with anger, "I fought hard to keep you after the first incident and then you go and do it again."

"But…"

She picked up a copy of the paper and threw it on the floor, "No 'buts' this time. Do you know the trouble you've caused me?"

Matt dropped his head in shame. "I'm sorry."

Julia stared out of the window. "God knows what this will do for my career."

"What happens now?" Matt asked, pretty sure of the answer.

She looked him right in the eye, "I'm afraid you're fired!"

Matt could feel his eyes filling up. He started to cry, "No, please Julia."

"I'm sorry there's nothing I can do," she turned to face the window, "you've brought it upon yourself."

This was the only time in her life that she had had to sack someone. It was not a pleasant experience, especially as she liked Matt, but she had to follow orders.

"You will be paid until the end of next month." Seeing Matt crying made her upset too. "You had better go now."

Matt got up, wiped the tears on his sleeve and took a moment to compose himself, before walking out of the bank for the final time. He kept his head bowed in shame, unable to face the other members of staff. Back in the office, Julia sat down and began to cry herself. That was the hardest task she had had to perform in her life. She was glad it was over.

Matt walked back to the pub to find Bully sitting down talking to Terry.

"When Julia told me what she had to do I asked to take the day off," he gave Matt a drink, "I couldn't bear to be there."

Terry kept the drinks flowing. Bully and Matt were drinking as if their lives depended on it, getting totally hammered. Neither spoke, only alcohol was consumed. Matt checked his watch: it was 2.45pm. Abbey would be waiting for him at the studio. He needed time to think.

"I'm going to the crematorium; I need to be alone for a while."

"Will you be all right?" Bully asked, showing concern for his best mate.

"Yes. I'll see you here about 7pm, and bring your guitar!"

Bully nodded. He asked Terry for a coffee: time to

start sobering up. Matt staggered to the exit and started the short journey to the crematorium.

Abbey and Craig arrived at the studio at 3.15pm. Craig did the introductions and they waited patiently for Matt to arrive. 3.25pm, 3.35pm and still no sign of him.

Paul checked his watch. "Doesn't look like he's coming, does it?" he looked at Abbey, "I'm sorry, love, I can't wait any longer. I've got an important meeting in ten minutes."

"I'm sorry to waste your valuable time." Abbey was extremely angry. "Come on Craig, I want to find him!"

"I'll catch you up; I just need to speak to Paul a minute."

Abbey left the room.

"Paul, I'm sorry. He's obviously nervous, but he's well worth the wait. Trust me, when he sung all the females hung on his every note!"

"We'll see. Phone me to make alternative arrangements if you find him. Now go."

Craig ran after Abbey and caught her up; she was on her mobile. "Damn! He's not home. We'll try the pub."

"What pub?" Craig asked, "Have you been there before?"

"Yes, The Swan. We'll need to get a taxi. Quick, there's one."

Bully was now sober after five cups of coffee. "I'd better go now, Terry, it's 4.30pm."

As he was leaving, Abbey and Craig entered. "Bully, where is he?"

"Well, well, well. If it isn't the lovers!"

"What are you going on about?" Abbey was in no mood for playing games.

"He overheard you two planning sex together. You're a bitch!"

That would explain his attitude yesterday.

"That's why he didn't turn up to the audition?"

"Audition? What audition?" Bully was getting more and more confused.

"Craig arranged an audition with his producer," Abbey continued, "Craig said that I had to sleep with him and he would arrange it. I tricked him into believing that I would, but I didn't, I swear."

Bully wasn't convinced. "Liar!"

"She's telling the truth, mate," Craig butted in. "She made me make the phone call then told everyone my plans. I was suitably chastised."

"I love Matt. I would never do that to him!"

"It's not me you have to convince," Bully added, "but I don't fancy your chances. He's at the crematorium."

"You go, Abbey, I need to do some bits and pieces." Craig smiled. "Good luck. Meet me at Sonya's."

They hugged and Abbey ran off to find Matt. Craig noticed the karaoke sign on the bar. "Will Matt be here tonight, mate?" he asked Bully. "Yes, I'm sure of it."

"Good. I'll get Paul, my producer, here to hear him sing." Craig looked around the bar. "Is there a phone I can use?"

Bully pointed to the far side of the bar. Craig chatted to someone briefly then put the phone down.

"Right. Paul will be here. All you need to do is get Matt to sing."

"Why are you doing this, Craig?"

"Because I could have ruined a good relationship by being a prat," there was a genuine tone of remorse in his voice. "Don't tell him though, it could ruin everything."

"No problem. My lips are sealed,"

"One other thing: where does he live?"

Bully looked puzzled but wrote down Matt's address, and told Craig how to get there. Whatever he had planned, he was risking a lot.

Abbey reached the crematorium. She walked to the plot where Matt's dad's ashes were. Matt was sitting on the bench where they had sat together on the last visit.

Matt glanced up, "What do you want?" His eyes were puffy: he had been crying.

"Why didn't you turn up for the audition?"

"I forgot about it, all right!" Matt replied, sharply, "I had other things on my mind."

"You made me look an idiot. I went out of my way to get you that audition."

"What, like sleeping with Craig?"

Abbey wondered when he would bring that up. "I didn't. I tricked him into believing I would."

"Bullshit!" Matt yelled. "I heard you talking."

"You only heard a small part of the conversation," Abbey resisted the temptation to yell back, staying calm, "Why would I sleep with him when I'm in love with someone else?" Matt looked puzzled. Was it Pat?

Before he could ask, Abbey answered, "With you Matt!"

Abbey finally admitted it to him. She felt a great sense of relief. Surely, he could see it.

"I wish I believed you," he said solemnly, "but I don't."

Abbey could not believe it. He was never going to change. Maybe she should admit defeat. "What have I got to do to prove it to you?"

Matt shrugged. Abbey was at her wit's end. Trying to convince him was an insurmountable task. "I can see that you're never going to change," she was heartbroken.

Abbey turned to leave. "You win. I'll get out of your life," her head dropped, "I can't go through life like this."

She admitted defeat and tears filled her eyes. She needed to get as far away from him as possible and move on, no matter how difficult it seemed.

Matt knew it was for the best; it would not work. She would never spend the rest of her life with him. There would come a day when she would get bored and move on. He watched as she walked out of his life, forever.

Matt arrived back at his flat at 5.30pm. The light was flashing on his answer phone, so he pressed the button.

'*You have one new message.*'

It was Abbey. 'If you're there, pick up', a long pause followed, 'Damn! He's not th—' She had put the phone down mid-sentence.

Matt was just about to jump in the shower, when there was a knock at the door.

"Whose there?"

No reply. He opened it to find Craig standing there.

"What do you want?" he asked abruptly. "Come to compare notes on Abbey?"

"I've come to talk some sense into you before it's too

late," Craig barged through the door. "I didn't sleep with Abbey, as much as I'd like to."

Matt slammed his door. "Why are you lying? I heard you both arranging it."

"Don't be an idiot!" Craig felt like shaking him. "You only heard a small part of the conversation."

"That was enough." Matt said defiantly.

"Am I going to have to physically knock some sense into you?"

"I'm not going to fight you, Craig!"

"Then fight for her, you idiot! Have you not noticed how Abbey hangs on your every word? How she looks at you?" he paused, "Remember when you were singing? She walked to the stage and stood there, staring at you. *She's in Love With You!*"

Matt thought back. Craig was right. He was enjoying the singing so much it did not register at the time. God! He had really blown it now.

"So what really happened?" Matt needed to know.

"It's not important!"

"It is to me."

Craig couldn't understand why but Matt wouldn't proceed until he had all the facts.

"Abbey tricked me into believing that she would sleep with me if I contacted my producer. Then she humiliated me in front of everyone by telling them what I tried to do."

"That was nasty." Matt felt for Craig. "Still, you deserved it!"

"Never mind that now, how do you feel about Abbey?"

Matt hesitated. "I… I worship her, but I don't feel it could work between us."

"How do you know? Don't you think she's worth the effort? You have nothing to lose and everything to gain."

Craig was right, but was it too late?

"What can I do, Craig?"

"I think you need to tell her you feel, then do something spectacular," he thought for a minute. "I know, sing to her; that worked before."

"They've got a karaoke tonight." Matt felt a glimmer of hope. "Trouble is, Abbey is unlikely to go there – we parted on bad terms."

"Leave that to me. You just concentrate on something amazing," Craig walked over to Matt and shook his hand, "Good luck. Remember: don't give up without a fight."

Craig left smiling. His plan was falling into place. All that remained now was to get Abbey to the pub. He hailed a taxi and gave the driver Sonya's address.

Abbey arrived at Sonya's an hour before and had not stopped crying since. She was distraught, but Sonya was there to comfort her.

"There's plenty more fish in the sea." The old cliché didn't help. "Come on, get ready, we're going out. Abbey wiped her eyes and went to have a wash. Craig knocked on the door and Sonya let him in. "We've got to get Abbey to the pub – I've made Matt see sense!"

"What are you going to tell her? He's changed his mind?"

"No. All we have to do is get her there. Matt will sort out the rest."

Sonya was delighted, but apprehensive. Would Matt be able to convince Abbey?

Abbey put on a pair of Sonya's jeans and a pink blouse. She thought it was pointless dressing up for a drink. She went downstairs to find Sonya deep in conversation with Craig.

"I think you should go and say good riddance to Matt tonight," Sonya suggested, "Show him what he's throwing away."

Abbey sighed, "Do I have to?"

Craig chipped in, "Just go there to say goodbye. Show him you're better than him."

"OK then."

She went into the kitchen for a drink. Sonya high-fived Craig. The last part of the plan was working. It was now all up to Matt.

19

Matt arrived at the pub at 6.55pm, but where was Bully? He was over the far side of the bar, talking to Terry.

He rushed over, "Bully, I need your help."

He told Bully of his plan. It would involve co-operation from the DJ, so Terry would sort that part out. Matt was going to perform, he would sort out anything.

Paul Sullivan slipped in unnoticed – it had become his trademark over the years – he could slip in and out of crowded rooms and nobody would know. He settled himself at the back of the room, where, experience told him, he would get the best view of the stage, and get the optimum sound output.

Bully started the evening. He decided to pick a number with a guitar solo in it as he had his with him. His performance was excellent. Paul wrote down his name and made a mental note of his appearance. The night had been worth it after all.

Bully now had the bug. He wanted to perform as often as possible. "Do a number with me, Matt."

"Not yet. I want to save myself for when Abbey gets here."

He looked at his watch: 7.30pm. Where were they? Sonya and Craig had decided that they should not go straight to the pub with Abbey, so they took her out for a meal. The restaurant they picked was extremely busy and it took an eternity to get a waitress to take their order. The starters came reasonably quickly. They shared a combination dish, which included chicken wings, covered in a barbecue sauce, mini corn on the cob, battered mushrooms, onion rings and croutons. They soon finished but after more than half an hour, there was still no sign of their main course. It was now 7.45pm. At this rate they would still be waiting at midnight. Craig excused himself from the table and went searching for their waitress. He found her rushing around, trying to do ten jobs at once.

"Excuse me," Craig turned on the charm, "could you give me an idea of when we can expect our main course? It's just that we need to be somewhere very soon."

He could tell that she had heard that line already tonight. "We are extremely busy, sir, as you can see."

"I appreciate that." He had to fight to keep his patience. "If you can give me some idea." He pulled out his wallet and discreetly handed over a handful of twenty pound notes and smiled.

She smiled at him. "I'll check for you."

Off she trotted to the kitchen and returned after a couple of minutes. "The chef estimates about ten to fifteen minutes."

"Thank you so much." He checked his watch again:

7.40pm. That meant they would be here until at least 8.30pm, which gave Matt more time. He hoped that Matt would still be there, but he had better phone to check.

The karaoke was a success: the bar was extremely busy. Terry had four staff working and he still needed to serve from time to time. Matt was ordering a drink when the phone rang.

"Grab that for us please, mate," Terry said to Matt.

He walked passed the staff – who were rushed off their feet – and went out the back to answer it.

"Hello…"

"Can you get a message to Matt Preston, please?"

"It's Matt speaking," he never received calls here, but he thought he recognised the voice, "Craig?"

"Don't panic, we will be there," Craig reassured him, "We're in a restaurant across town and should be there about 9pm. Got to go, or Abbey will be suspicious."

He hung up the phone. Matt was relieved to hear from Craig but now felt extremely nervous as he knew how much longer he would have to wait.

Craig returned to the table. Abbey and Sonya were busily chatting to each other.

Abbey looked up, "Where have you been all this time?"

"Trying to find out how much longer we're going to have to wait."

Sonya looked a little concerned. "How long?"

"About another fifteen minutes." He gave her a reassuring look. "This might be it now…" The waitress was carrying a large tray, with, at last, their food. Sonya had a lasagne, Abbey had chicken with a jacket potato and Craig had steak and chips.

"Enjoy your meals," the waitress was much rehearsed, "can I get you any more drinks?"

They ordered three cokes, not giving Abbey the chance to order anything else. They wanted to get her to the pub as quickly as possible.

Bully just finished his third number. He rejoined Matt at the table. "Still no sign then?"

"I've just spoken to Craig," he said, swallowing his nerves, "They'll probably get here around 9pm."

"What song have you got planned?" Bully was curious.

"'Me and Mrs Jones' – quite apt, don't you think?"

"What if that doesn't work?" Bully's optimism shining through.

"I have a back up, but that's a secret. All you need to do is keep her here."

"No worries!"

For him, maybe – Matt was terrified. He kept playing with a beer mat, flicking it up into the air then trying to catch it, anything to keep his mind occupied. He was shortly to face with the most crucial ten minutes of his life, so there was no room for error.

Paul went to the bar to order a drink. Where was Craig? When would Matt sing? "Orange juice and lemonade, please, pint." He paid the bartender, went back to his spot, and watched as another group were singing, or rather screaming.

Paul hated these nights, being subjected to a bunch

of talentless individuals, ruining classic songs. *Karaoke should be banned*, he thought.

Craig checked his watch: it was 8.50pm. Why did it take women so long to eat? Sonya and Abbey had spent most of the time talking instead of eating. At this rate, they would be arriving at the pub just before closing time. He had not planned for this setback.

"I think I want to just go back to Sonya's," Abbey stated, "I don't think I can be bothered to see him."

Craig and Sonya stared at each other, panic setting in.

"So you'll let him think he's won?" Sonya chipped in quickly.

"Sonya's right," Craig backed her up, "Show him it doesn't bother you."

"Well if you think that's the best move."

They both breathed a sigh of relief. *Thank Christ for that*, Craig thought.

The waitress returned to the table. "Have you finished?"

Craig prayed that Abbey would be full and not waste more time by ordering a dessert.

"Would you like to see the dessert menu?"

"No!" Sonya replied rapidly. "Let's get this meeting out of the way so we can go home."

Abbey agreed, much to their relief. The waitress returned with the bill for £120. Sonya pulled a bunch of twenties from her purse and gave them to the waitress. They were ready to leave.

"Keep the change, we are in a hurry!"

Outside the streets were extremely busy; trying to find a taxi would prove to be a problem. They walked up and down the street several times but no taxis were available. A stroke of luck! A taxi pulled up right in front of them, dropping off a couple that were about to dine at the restaurant. They piled inside the cab and were at last they were on their way.

Terry came over to Matt. "Are you sure she's going to turn up? It's 9.30pm!"

"Craig said that he would get her here." Matt was more relaxed after a couple of pints of 'Dutch courage'.

Bully kept his eyes fixed on the doorway. He promised Matt that he would not do any more numbers so he could chase after Abbey if she ran off.

The taxi pulled up outside the pub. Craig paid the fare while Abbey and Sonya climbed out.

"Now, Abbey, keep calm and don't lose your temper," Sonya gave her a hug, "after this you can get on with your life, girl."

"I'll be fine," Abbey sounded confident, "I won't waste any more time thinking about him. I know it will be hard, but I won't have to see him after tonight."

Sonya opened the door. A cloud of cigarette smoke hit them, and then escaped into the night's sky. Inside was it was so dark that it was extremely difficult to recognise anyone. They scanned the room, starting in different directions and meeting in the middle.

Sonya spotted Bully and tapped Abbey on the

shoulder. "They're over there. Good luck." Abbey made her way over to the table.

"Shit! Here she comes, Matt."

Matt tensed up. It was now or never. Bully gave the signal to Terry, who, in turn, gave the thumbs up.

Abbey stopped in front of the Matt and Bully. "You were right, Matt, and I've just come to say goodbye."

"No, Abbey I've been a prat – a blind, stupid prat!"

"It's too late now, you've had your chance." She turned to leave.

Matt grabbed her arm, stopping her in her tracks. "Hear me out, please!"

She shook free of his grasp, folded her arms and waited for his response.

"I love you, I always have. I just couldn't believe that someone like you could love me back."

Abbey looked unimpressed. "It's not enough. It's too little, too late. Your insecurity won't allow you to ever be happy."

Terry interrupted the conversation with an announcement, "Our next singer is somewhat of a celebrity. Please put your hands together for Matt."

Applause broke out, everyone's attention focused on him.

"Abbey, please don't go. Wait!" He was begging her.

He walked up to the stage and wheeled the piano forward, arranging it so he could see into the crowd. He was not going to use the karaoke machine. He moved the microphone and stand over to the piano and adjusted the height so that he could sing and play at the same time.

Paul's ears pricked up when he heard the name. *At last!* This is what he had been waiting for all night. Craig joined him with Sonya in tow.

Matt started to shake. "Stop it!" he told himself, "It was no different to before, in Manchester."

He sat down, positioning his hands over the keys to start. He cleared his throat: it felt so dry. All the moisture in his mouth has disappeared, so he sipped his lager.

"Thank you," he practiced the introduction, "This song is close to my heart."

He glanced over in Abbey's direction, and she was still there. He started playing, his hands gliding over the keys. *So far so good.* He took a deep breath, "Me and Abbey Jones."

Abbey smiled, he sounded good. She looked around for the others, but they were over by the back wall. She made her way over to them. Matt saw her go, and anxiously watched her walk away. Bully followed to ensure she wasn't leaving.

As Abbey drew closer to them, she spotted Paul. How did he know Matt would be here? She glanced over to Craig. He was grinning from ear to ear. He must have arranged it.

"I felt it was the least I could do," he said sincerely, "after all, it was my fault you didn't get together."

Abbey gave him a hug, "Thanks, Craig." She turned to Paul, "Well, what do you think?"

"Not bad," he smiled, "In fact, very good. Like the alteration of the words."

Matt carried on singing, throwing all his effort into the song. He closed his eyes, hoping Abbey would come running over to him. As far as he could tell she was still here, but he could not be sure.

Bully caught up with Abbey. “He really loves you, he just struggles with words. This is his way of telling you.”

“It will take more than a song to win me back,” she yelled angrily. “I can’t live my life with his unpredictability.”

“Give him a break,” Bully pleaded, “Every women he’s been with has shit on him, no wonder he’s like he is.”

“Maybe,” Abbey stared at Matt, “but he’ll have to do something really special to convince me.”

Matt was coming to the end of the song. He spotted Bully at the back of the room. He finished singing and the whole place erupted. Terry walked over to Matt with a broad smile on his face.

“That was fantastic, man, brilliant.”

Matt glanced over in Bully’s direction. He was shaking his head, the signal that she was not convinced, “Terry, I need to do another one.”

“Go on, knock ‘em dead!” He rejoined the front of the crowd who were still applauding.

“Thank you so much,” Matt played about on the piano, “I’d like to do another song dedicated to the girl I love! I’m not very good with words, but I hope this song expresses what you mean to me, Abbey.”

All eyes turned to Abbey. She became extremely embarrassed, as Craig patted her on the back and cheered. Silence fell around the room, everyone waiting for Matt to start. He recalled the song in his mind and started to play, but suddenly stopped. Abbey shook her head, turned round and tried to leave but Sonya grabbed her arm, holding her tightly.

"Wait a minute," he looked up, "Bully, come here."

Bully ran through the crowd to the piano, "What, mate?"

"Remember at Mandy's wedding…?"

"Yes."

"We're going to do it again and you're going to play the piano."

"I haven't for ages, but I'll try not to fuck it up."

"I know you won't. Can you remember how it goes?"

"Yep. This had better be good; she's trying to leave! Ready?"

Matt nodded. Abbey broke free from Sonya's clutches and started once more for the exit . Bully started to play. Abbey instantly recognised the song: he was going to sing 'Mandy'. She felt a chill run down her spine. She froze unable to leave, the music paralysing her.

This was a thousand times better than before. Abbey could feel the hairs on the back of her neck standing on end again. She was so moved. No one had ever gone to this extent to win her love. He even sang her name in place of Mandy. The tears were welling up in her eyes; they would soon be cascading down her cheeks. She turned round to face the front of the room again.

Sonya looked around the room. All the females were so engrossed, wishing that Matt was singing to them. Her attention switched to Abbey. She noticed the tears. *It's working*, she thought!

Matt had never seen the pub like this before. Everyone in the room had stopped what they were doing and watched him. He could get used to this.

Matt started to walk through the crowd in Abbey's

direction. They parted, clearing a path directly to her.

"Go for it, my son!" Bully yelled from the piano. Matt walked past Terry, who extended his hand and nodded his approval. Matt was closing in on his prey. Tears were still trickling down Abbey's cheeks, and the crowd's eyes were shifting towards her as Matt passed them. People patted him on the back as he arrived in front of Abbey. He extended his right hand to wipe away the tears from her eyes.

He took another deep breath and carried on singing with a broad smile on his face. She remained fixed to the spot. Matt dropped to his knees and stretched out his free hand and clutched Abbey's right hand, gently stroking it with his thumb. More tears ran down her cheeks. She hurriedly wiped them away, and smiled. She grabbed Matt's shirt and pulled him to his feet, into her arms.

As she kissed him, the crowd went berserk, whistling and cheering.

Matt pulled away from her kiss and moved his lips to her ear. "I'm sorry, I will never doubt you again."

Abbey wiped away a fresh set of tears. "I love you so much. I want to spend the rest of my life with you!"

They kissed again and the crowd started clapping again. Bully finished playing and ran over to them, grabbing them both in a big clinch. "Well done, my son!"

Abbey turned to face Paul. "How about that then?"

"That was absolutely magnificent! I want to sign both of you." He pointed to Bully as well as Matt.

They looked at each other in amazement, hugged and started jumping about as if they had won the lottery.

Matt turned back to Abbey, "Thank you, I'm forever in your debt."

Abbey looked embarrassed. "Actually I had nothing to do with it this time."

Craig stepped forward. "I arranged it. It was the least I could do after all the trouble I've caused."

Matt shook him by the hand. "You're all right really."

Terry came walking over, "I hate to break up this joyous moment but there are people who want to continue the karaoke."

They looked at Matt; he was still clutching the microphone. He handed it back to Terry.

Paul finished his drink and placed the empty glass on a table. "Right then, you two," he pulled Bully and Matt to one side, "come to my office on Monday and we'll discuss contracts, OK?" He shook their hands and said his goodbyes. Craig followed him to the door to see him off.

"Right! Let's celebrate!" Sonya, who had been quiet until now, wanted to make up for lost time.

She grabbed Bully by the arm. "Fancy a drink?"

After an initial look of shock he smiled and Sonya yanked him on his way. He turned his head towards Matt and Abbey and mouthed wow! They both laughed and Matt gave Abbey another tight squeeze. He never wanted to let her go. Abbey broke free and took his hand and pulled him in the direction of the bar to join Sonya and Bully. They ordered a round of drinks and turned to watch the continuance of the karaoke. Occasionally, the odd person would approach them for Abbey's autograph or to congratulate the lads on their respective performances.

After a short period of time Matt grabbed Abbey by the hand and led her outside. He stopped and wrapped his arms around her, and gave her a big hug, squeezing her tightly. He gazed deep into her eyes.

"Am I dreaming?" he asked. "I can't believe what's happening! I have just won the heart of one of the most beautiful woman I have ever seen and I have been offered a recording contract."

"Shut up and kiss me!" Abbey demanded.

He did not disappoint. He placed his hand on her cheek and kissed her, slowly. She rubbed her hands up and down his back. After a couple of minutes of passionate kissing, Abbey backed off.

"We'd better go back and join the others; we've got all night to continue this." She raised her eyebrows and smiled. Matt got the message. He was about to have the night of his life!

Epilogue

"Bully here. Well, what a turn of events over the last couple of weeks. I can't quite believe it myself. The girl of Matt's dreams actually falling in love with him, then he nearly blows it, only to win her back by singing her favourite song. A record producer hears us perform, likes us, and wants to sign us. It's all too much to take in!

Now I find out that Sonya's writing a book based on the events. Can't wait to read it. What interests me more is what happens next. Will they stay together? Will Sonya and me become an item, and will we be successful? If you are that type of person, write in, and maybe you'll find out. All I can say is, ladies and gentlemen, it's up to you.

Oh, and… the end, for now!"